● ● ● ● ● ●

Asha didn't think she'd ever been more shook. She placed her cellphone on the table and then her purse. She began to remove the items from it, and he told her, "Just turn it upside down and dump it out."

She had no choice but to comply.

The man reached for his electronic device. He pressed a button on the side, and a small, green light came on. He lifted the wand and slowly passed it over her phone and the contents of her purse. Nothing happened. He made another pass and got the same results. Asha realized he was looking for a wiretap. Her eyes widened as she looked up at him. Outside of a movie, she had never seen anything like this. Who the hell was this man?

He stepped around the table and used the wand to sweep her whole body at the same, mind numbing pace. His closeness made her heart pound even harder. After scanning her front, he told her, "Turn around," and began to scan her back, from head to toe. Finally satisfied, he took a step back and said, "Alright, you can turn back around."

Asha tried to hide her fear as she turned his way again. "Everything cool?" she asked. She knew he hadn't found anything, but she was desperate for his approval.

He placed the wand on the table and nodded. "You can put your stuff back in your purse."

Asha didn't think he'd give her an answer, but as she gathered her things, she asked, "Can you tell me why the music up so loud?"

He told her, "Just because you ain't bugged don't mean you ain't got the laws parked around the corner in a surveillance van."

Once again, Asha had never seen a surveillance van outside of TV. She knew they had high-tech listening devices that could pick up a conversation from blocks away. The fact that this man had a tactic to thwart this let her know that he was the real deal; a professional killer, and he was looking out for her safety as much as he was looking out for himself.

At that moment, she knew she was hiring the right man for the job.

● ● ● ● ● ●

ASHA AND BOOM PART 1

KEITH THOMAS WALKER

KEITHWALKERBOOKS, INC
This is a UMS production

KEITHWALKERBOOKS

Publishing Company
KeithWalkerBooks, Inc.
P.O. Box 690
Allen, TX 75013

For information write
KeithWalkerBooks, Inc.
P.O. Box 690
Allen, TX 75013

ISBN-13 DIGIT: 978-1-7320624-9-8
ISBN-10 DIGIT: 1-7320624-9-8
Library of Congress Control Number: 2020913904
Manufactured in the United States of America

Second Edition

Visit us at www.keithwalkerbooks.com

This book is for my rose Wynema

MORE BOOKS BY
KEITH THOMAS WALKER

Fixin' Tyrone
How to Kill Your Husband
A Good Dude
Riding the Corporate Ladder
The Finley Sisters' Oath of Romance
Blow by Blow
Jewell and the Dapper Dan
Harlot
Plan C (And More KWB Shorts)
Dripping Chocolate
The Realest Ever
Jackson Memorial
Sleeping With the Strangler
Life After
Blood for Isaiah
Brick House
Brick House 2
One on One
Brick House 3
Jackson Memorial 2
Backslide
Threesome
Backslide 2
Threesome 2
Election Day
Evan's Heart

NOVELLAS

Might be Bi Part One
Harder

Primal Part One
The Realest Christmas Ever
Hotline Fling

POETRY COLLECTION

Poor Righteous Poet

FINLEY HIGH SERIES

Prom Night at Finley High
Fast Girls at Finley High
Bullies at Finley High

Visit www.keithwalkerbooks.com for information about these and upcoming titles from KeithWalkerBooks

ACKNOWLEDGMENTS

Of course I would like to thank God, first and foremost, for giving me the creativity and drive to pursue my dreams and the understanding that I am nothing without Him. I would like to thank my beautiful wife and my mother for always pushing me to be the best I can be. I would like to thank Janae Hafford for being the best advisor, supporter and little sister a brother could ever have.

I would also like to thank (in no particular order) Beulah Neveu, Deloris Harper, Denise Fizer, Michele Halsey Hallahan, Priscilla C. Johnson, Kim Tanner, Tia Kelly, Edwina Putney, Melissa Carter, Cathy Atchison, Lanita Irvin, Ramona Weathersbee, Cynthia Antoinette Taylor, Jason Owens, Ramona Brown, Johnathan Royal, Sharon Blount, BRAB Book Club, and Uncle Steven Thomas, one love. I'd like to thank everyone who purchased and enjoyed one of my books. Everything I do has always been to please you. I know there are folks who mean the world to me that I'm failing to mention. I apologize ahead of time. Rest assured I'm grateful for everything you've done for me!

CHAPTER ONE
REPAST

As a rule, Asha never looked into coffins at funerals. She understood why the practice was necessary for some. But for her, the image only served to sully an otherwise pleasant memory of her loved one.

The option was never under consideration for Lil Richey's service, so she was spared the torment of seeing her nephew one last time. Due to his small body lying undiscovered for a little over a week, coupled with other trauma his killer had inflicted, the funeral home decided a closed casket service would be more appropriate, and his mother agreed. Asha's sister, Gloria, was as tormented as Emmett Till's mother, but she was not of the mindset that the world needed to see what happened to her baby.

Asha sat alone on the bleachers at the Hemphill Community Center, where the family had chosen to hold the

9

repast. Gloria's church had offered to host the gathering, but Emmanuel Baptist was a small building, and Lil Richey's murder was national news. There were more than 200 mourners and over a dozen reporters at his funeral. The crowd hadn't dwindled much since they transitioned to the community center.

The gymnasium smelled of fried chicken, butter rolls, pot roast and an assortment of pies that were set up in an adjacent game room that had been converted into a feeding area. The crowd moved from there to the gym, where they toted their paper plates and Styrofoam cups and conversed quietly. There were scarcely any smiles, even from the multitude of children dressed in their formal wear, who wished someone would bring out one of the basketballs that were racked behind the check-in desk. The gym had six perfectly good hoops mounted overhead. Why not let them kick off their church shoes and play with at least one of them?

Asha did not have a plate or Styrofoam cup in hand. She sat stoically, staring at the horde of people, but not really seeing any of them. Never one for dresses, she wore a black pantsuit with a white blouse. Her hair was shoulder length with frizzy curls. Her skin tone was very fair. Her eyes were bloodshot. They were dry but glossy at the moment. Tear stains left salt streaks down her cheeks. The smell of good cooking made her nauseous. She rose to her feet just as her sister's pastor approached her. His features were comforting, as were his soft eyes, lined with crow's-feet in the corners.

"Sister Asha..."

His hands were clasped together. Asha watched as they separated, and he reached for hers. She offered a hand

and stared numbly as he enveloped it with his weathered paws.

"How you holding up?" he asked with a soft voice that was still robust.

She shrugged, looking into his eyes.

"I know this is a difficult time for you," he said, "but the Lord promises a rainbow after every storm. This world we live in is full of torment and pain. As hard as it is to let him go, there's no doubt Richey is in a better place."

The pastor had already offered this assessment during his eulogy. It didn't make Asha feel any better then, and it didn't help now. The last time she saw Lil Richey, he was as happy and vivacious as any five-year-old child, just a few months shy of his sixth birthday. Asha couldn't see how death was a better alternative to the many years of life and laughter that were brutally taken away from him – even if his death opened the gates of heaven.

"Do you mind if I pray for you?" the pastor asked.

Asha didn't respond, but he began his prayer just the same. She didn't intentionally tune him out as he spoke, but her gaze wandered and settled on the large mural that hung near the entrance of the gym. In addition to a larger than life picture of her nephew, the mural depicted images of his favorite things; soccer balls, basketballs, Hot wheels and Paw Patrol characters. A few people were standing before the mural, adding their goodbyes with one of the Sharpies the community center provided for well-wishers.

Asha's eyes returned to the pastor, who was still praying, his head bowed. It was not lost on her that Lil Richey would still be with them today if another pastor hadn't actually been a demon in disguise. She waited for the man of God to release her and say, "*Amen.*" Her head began to spin when the prayer didn't end quickly enough.

She withdrew her hand and said, "I'm sorry, Pastor, but I have to go. I don't feel good. I need some fresh air."

The older man's demeanor was awash with sorrow. He nodded.

"Okay, sister. Please come and find me when you come back in."

"Okay, I will."

She stepped past him and managed to make it to the front of the gym without anyone else stopping her. She paused at Lil Richey's mural before she exited the gym. Other than the graphics, it was blank when she first arrived at the community center. Now it had nearly a hundred messages Richey could presumably read from heaven. Asha had yet to write anything on the mural, but she hoped to find the strength to do so before the repast ended.

Outside, the sunlight was initially blinding, the heat equally stifling. With the July temperatures roaring past 100, the safe confines of the airconditioned community center was the only logical option, but Asha heard a few voices in the packed parking lot. She gravitated towards the sound and caught a whiff of cigarette smoke as she neared a small crowd of faces she recognized. They were all relatives, with the exception of the lone female. But Tristan had been with his baby-mama for so long, Asha considered Courtney family.

She stepped to the group and posted up next to her uncle's Escalade. Her cousin Tristan sat in his Mustang with the door open. His girlfriend leaned next to him on the sleek, black ride. Asha's other cousins Cedric and Broderick were there, along with her stepbrother Henry. Uncle Lucius sat in the open door of his SUV. Though all of them were sweating, their reason for being outside was apparent. Three of the men were smoking, and Tristan cradled a bottle of Johnny Walker Blue Label.

"What's up, Asha," he said and offered her the bottle.

She stepped forward and took it from him. Though her stomach was unsettled, and she'd never had a good experience with drinking in the heat, she turned the bottle up like she was at a house party. No one questioned the two man-size gulps she took before handing the bottle back to Tristan, but her uncle reached for it instead.

"Let me get that."

She gave it to him and returned to her spot next to his Escalade.

Tristan watched her for a few beats before saying, "We out here talking about that pastor. You know he bonded hisself out last night..."

Asha nodded slightly.

"How the hell that motherfucker even get a bond?" Lucius wondered. "They should've threw that pervert up *under* the jail. Ain't nobody who did that shit to some little kid should be walking around right now like a free man."

Most of the people inside the community center would've found Lucius' vitriol poisonous and self-defeating, especially on the day they laid Lil Richey to rest. But Asha

13

had been waiting for someone to give voice to the torment in her heart.

"They didn't have enough evidence to give him a higher bond," she told him. "They barely had enough to arrest his ass."

"They got that nigga on camera with Lil Richey in his car," Lucius countered. "They got that video right after church camp ended that day. He ain't have no business with my nephew in his damn car."

"But that's all they got," Cedric said. "They didn't find nothing in his house, and they didn't find no evidence when they found Richey. This ain't no strong case. It's circumstantial."

"The hell it is!" Lucius barked. "My nephew been going to that church for years, sitting in class with that motherfucker. Supposed to be hearing the word of God, but that molester prolly been peeping him the whole time, waiting for his chance to snatch him. He drive off church property with Richey in his car and don't say shit about it for a week, while the whole city looking for him. You trying to say he ain't do that shit?"

The look in Lucius' eyes and the bulk of his frame would've made anyone agree to whatever he wanted them to, but Cedric didn't need convincing.

"Naw, I ain't saying that. I *know* he killed Richey."

"He didn't just kill him," Lucius interjected. "He fucking *raped* him."

Those words continued to make Asha's body numb, no matter how many times she heard them.

"I'm just saying what them white folks on TV was saying," Cedric continued. "They say it's a weak case, and that's why they couldn't give him no high bond."

"That's *buuullshit*," Lucius exclaimed. "White folks always looking out for each other, even if they protecting a goddamned pervert! You know they taking it easy on him, 'cause he white, and he a pastor."

"It ain't that," Asha said, shaking her head. "I saw it on TV too. Him driving off with Lil Richey don't prove he killed him."

Before Lucius' response could catch up to his frown, Asha said, "I ain't saying he didn't do it, either. Everybody know he did it. Some other kids done came forward, talking about how he used to make comments and make them feel uncomfortable. But they don't have enough evidence for this to be open and shut. That's why they only arrested him for kidnapping and not murder. The DA said she's hoping the detectives find more evidence, so they can hit him with another charge."

"What if they don't?" Tristan pondered. "What if what they got is all they gon' get? They convict him of kidnapping, and he get what, like ten years? My little nigga gone, and that motherfucker get off?"

Tristan was rough around the edges, but the circumstances surrounding Richey's death could make even the scariest goon tear up. He wiped the sweat from his forehead and the tears from his eyes with one palm sliding down his face.

"I don't think he gon' get off," Courtney said. "You can't do everything he did to Richey without leaving *some* kind of evidence. They gon' find it, and when they do, they gon' burn his ass."

Asha nodded, slightly comforted by those sentiments. She was also comforted by the liquor that was now coursing through her bloodstream. She knew she'd regret it later, but

15

she reached for the bottle again. "Gimme some more of that."

Lucius handed it to her. "You want a square too?" He produced a pack of Newport's.

Asha hadn't smoked since before she got locked up, but she told him, "Shit, might as well."

A few moments later, the headrush from the cigarette collided with the alcohol and the heat, and she leaned even heavier on the hot Escalade.

"You alright?" her uncle asked.

She shook her head, her tears falling anew. "Naw." Her eyes slipped closed. "I don't think I'm gon' be alright until that man is convicted of murder. I wish somebody would've killed him when he got locked up. How they let him slip through like that?"

"He was probably in protective custody," Lucius said knowingly. Other than Tristan and his woman, everyone in the group had wasted away a number of years in prison.

"If they don't get him for murder, I'm liable to kill his ass myself," Asha said, mainly to herself. Her declaration caused an uneasy silence to settle among the group.

Tristan broke it by saying, "You, Asha you just got out. You shouldn't be talking like that."

She opened her eyes and stared at him. "I'm serious. You don't think he deserve to die for what he did to Richey?"

"I ain't saying he don't."

"But you wouldn't do it yourself?"

She knew she was asking the wrong person. Tristan's small-time drug dealing led to a few arrests for possession and assault, but hadn't even graduated to *aggravated* assault, let alone murder.

"I'm, I mean, if I was to do something like that, I wouldn't do it myself. I'd probably hire somebody. I wouldn't get my hands dirty like that."

Asha continued to stare at him, her eyes cold now. "Hire somebody? Like who? You know somebody who get down like that?"

He shook his head. "No, not *personally*. But I know some people who know somebody." His eyes narrowed as he watched his cousin. "But you shouldn't be thinking about nothing like that either. Them laws ain't through with that man. I bet in a couple of—"

"Hey, what y'all doing out here?"

Everyone looked back, surprised that someone had gotten so close without them hearing. When they saw who it was, they straightened their postures and put away the liquor, as if it was the police. Gloria warranted this respect, because none of the pain they felt was comparable to the anguish Richey's mother had been through. Asha's heart bled for her sister the moment they locked eyes.

When no one responded to her, Gloria singled out the person she was closest to.

"Asha, what's going on? Why you out here?"

Asha shrugged. "Nothing, we just..." She shook her head. "We just, we just chilling."

Gloria looked down at the cigarette in her hand before eyeing the people she was talking to. "Can you come back inside?" she asked her sister. "I need to talk to you."

Asha nodded. She pushed off the car and dropped her cigarette.

"How you doing, G?" Lucius asked. "You know we all praying for you."

17

"I'm okay, Uncle," Gloria replied. "It's day-to-day. Today's been the hardest one so far. They keep saying things will get better, but I don't see how."

Asha and her sister weren't physically similar. Mentally they were worlds apart as well. Gloria wore the look of a mother whose worst fear had been realized. During the week Lil Richey was missing, Asha had watched her beautiful spirit slowly wither away, as if it was being decimated by locusts. What stood before them now was a shell of the woman they had once known. Not only had Gloria lost weight, but she seemed to have aged ten years. Asha wondered if her sister would ever experience the true joy she had known before Richey was first reported missing.

"We here for you, if you ever need anything," Courtney said.

"Yeah, we all are," Cedric tacked on.

Gloria nodded and offered a cursory, "Thank you," before turning towards the community center.

Asha wiped the sweat off her brow as she followed her.

Inside the community center, Asha was greeted with cool, refreshing temperatures that made her wonder why she ever thought the sizzling heat was a better alternative. Gloria headed for one of the unoccupied weight rooms, rather than speak to her sister publicly. One of the staff members moved to cut her off, but she stopped short when she saw who it was.

"Oh, um, Mrs. Turner, you would like to use this room?"

"Yes, just for a minute. Is it alright?"

"Yes, of course," the woman said. She quickly searched for the appropriate key on a keychain affixed to her belt. She unlocked the door and held it open for Asha and Gloria to enter. "If you need anything else," she said, "please don't hesitate to let me know."

"Thank you," Gloria said, without looking back.

Asha waited for the staff member to add the perfunctory, "I'm sorry for your loss," but the girl didn't.

The weight room had glass doors and walls, but with the door closed, their conversation was relatively private. Gloria turned to face her.

"How you feeling?"

Asha shook her head. "I'm the one who should be asking you that."

"You've been worried about me for the past ten days," Gloria replied. "I think it's time for me to start looking out for other people."

Asha continued to shake her head. "No, it's not. That's the last thing you need to be doing right now."

Gloria sighed. "Yeah, it is, Asha. I still have a husband, two kids... And I've got you, and everyone else I care about. I need to know that you're okay. I'm worried about you."

Her compassion broke Asha's heart and made her sick to her stomach. Her eyes were almost pleading when she said, "G, everybody in this building needs to be worried about you, not the other way around."

Never one to mince words, Gloria said, "Asha, I heard what y'all were talking about out there."

Asha's emotional bank was nearly depleted. She didn't have enough empathy to feign guilt.

"Why were you out there talking to them anyway?" Gloria wondered. "Not one of them has anything constructive to say at a time like this."

Asha frowned. "They family, Sis. Just because they not in here crying don't mean what they have to say doesn't matter."

"What did they have to say, Asha? *How they let that motherfucker go?* And *Somebody need to kill that motherfucker...*"

Asha's mouth fell open, but a moment passed before she could respond. "And what's wrong with that? Somebody does need to take care of him. If it's ever been a time to kill, I know you know this is it."

Gloria brought a hand to her face and rubbed between her eyes. When she withdrew her hand, her eyes were once again filled with tears. For the life of her, Asha couldn't understand how her sister could possibly have any tears left.

"Do you remember when I came to that prison and asked if you were willing to be Richey's godmother?" Gloria asked.

Asha nodded. "Of course I remember. It was one of the best days of my life. I cried so hard when you were there and kept crying when you left."

"Do you remember why I made that decision?"

Asha did remember, but she didn't respond.

"I told you that being responsible for another life," Gloria said, "if something were to ever happen to me and Richard, should give you something to live for, a reason to do the right thing when you got out. You promised me you would never do anything to get you sent back to that place." Her breaths came in shudders while she waited for her sister to respond, but Asha remained mute.

"So," Gloria continued, "since Richey's gone, you feel like you don't have to keep that promise anymore? Was he the only reason you worked hard and bought a car, got your own place?"

Asha shook her head, her tears falling as well.

"Then why would you be out there talking about stuff like that on the day my son got put in the ground – the day your godson was buried?"

Asha was surprised to see anger in her sister's wet orbs.

"If you loved Richey, like I *know* you did, you wouldn't disrespect his memory by talking about *murder*. If he had anything to do with the transformation you made when you got out, then the best thing you can do right now is honor him by continuing on the path you started. *That's* something you can do in his name. You out there drinking and smoking an hour after we buried my son... That's not you, Asha. You know it's not."

Asha thought she didn't have the wherewithal to register shame, but she was wrong.

"I'm sorry, G," she said sobbing. "I'm sorry you heard any of that."

"Don't be sorry that I heard it, be sorry that y'all were thinking it. I need you to promise me that that conversation is over. That man will get the punishment he deserves. You don't have to lift a finger to do God's work."

Asha nodded. She couldn't stop her tears from falling. Neither of them could.

"I promise, Sis. I'm sorry."

They came together and held each other for what felt like an eternity. Eventually, they rejoined the repast hand-in-hand.

Asha remained at the service until the sun was starting to set and everyone said their goodbyes. She got the prayer the pastor was so insistent on, and she made sure to sign Lil Richey's mural before they rolled it up and delivered it to his mother.

She wrote:

> I know that your soul is at peace
> and I can't wait to see you again in the
> afterlife. You will always be in my heart.
> I love you more than words can say
> Asha

When she made it to the parking lot, Asha spent another twenty minutes offering and receiving more hugs from relatives and well-wishers. When she finally broke away from them and headed to her car, she was surprised to see Tristan was still there. She approached his Mustang, and her cousin rolled his window down. Courtney sat next to him on the passenger side. The car reeked of marijuana, but there was no greenery currently lit.

"What's up, Asha?" Tristan called. "You get in trouble with G earlier?"

"Naw," Asha said, but she looked over her shoulder to make sure her sister wasn't creeping up on her again. "It's all good. Where you headed?"

"To the house," Tristan said. "Gotta pick the kids up from her sister's first. Why, what's up?"

"I need to holler at you," Asha told him. "Can you roll with me? I'll drop you off at your place when we're done."

She was surprised by the look of foreboding that washed over her cousin's face before he looked at his woman and said, "Say, I'ma meet you at the house in a little bit."

Courtney told him, "Okay."

They both opened their doors and exited the vehicle. Courtney moved to the driver's side, and Tristan followed Asha to her truck.

CHAPTER TWO
MR. LUCK

Asha piloted her F-150 in the general direction of Tristan's apartment on the south side of town. She drove slowly, to make sure they'd have time to talk before they arrived at their destination. Casual glances at her passenger revealed he was as anxious as he was when she approached his car a few minutes ago.

"What you trippin' on?" she finally asked him.

"Nothing," he said, his attention diverted. Tristan was a caramel colored pretty boy with hood features; long hair, tats on his arms, chest and up to his neck.

Asha frowned at him. "You staring out the window like you just got off a plane or something. What you nervous about?"

He shook his head. "I ain't nervous." He then asked, "What G say to you when she came out there earlier?"

Asha's eyes moved back to the road. "That's what got you shook? She didn't even say nothing to you."

"I know, but I was wondering if she heard what we was talking about."

"Why you worried about that?"

"Because I know that's what you wanna talk to me about, and I don't like the idea of G knowing about it. That's how niggas get caught up. I ain't saying she a snitch or nothing, but you know your sister ain't like us. I wish I never said nothing, with all them people out there. Something happen to that pastor, it's five or six people who can give them laws a lead. You should be worried about that too, if that's where your mind's at right now..."

Asha was surprised by her cousin's wariness. She had always assumed Tristan avoided the penitentiary because he didn't get involved in anything too serious. Maybe he had avoided those high fences and barbed wire because he was consistently careful.

"She heard what we was talking about?" he asked again.

"Yeah," Asha conceded, "but not about hiring nobody. All she heard was we think somebody should kill that pastor. Prolly half the people that heard about what happened to Lil Richey feel that way."

"What she tell you?"

"She said it wasn't good to talk like that, and I promised her I'd let it go."

Tristan nodded. "I think that's a promise you should keep."

Asha's frown intensified. "So now you wanna let it go? That ain't what you said earlier."

"I told you the same thing I'm telling you now," Tristan countered. "I told you as bad as I want that man dead, I wouldn't get my hands dirty like that. I said you shouldn't either. Ain't nothing I said changed."

"That's why Zimmerman walking around right now, 'cause of do-nothing niggas like you," Asha said with a sneer.

Tristan sneered right back at her. "What I got to do with that?"

"Shit, nothing, I guess. Just like every other nigga out here had so much to say about Trayvon, but when Zimmerman walked out that court, ain't nobody did shit. I guess you wanna wait for *God* to get justice for Lil Richey..."

Tristan continued to stare at her.

"You don't even gotta do shit," Asha said. "You said you know somebody that know somebody... Put me in contact with them, and I'll take care of it myself."

They stopped at a light, and she turned to look at her cousin. Tristan was fuming. Her expression softened. The way she was speaking to him was bad enough. The implication that she was a female with more heart than him was certainly emasculating.

"I ain't trying to say you don't handle your business," she told him. "I understand why you don't wanna get involved with this. You and Courtney got little kids to look after. I'm just asking you to pass me along to the right people."

"I do wanna do something about that pastor," Tristan said. "But the dude I'm talking about wouldn't do it for anything less than twenty racks. I ain't got the paper to hire that man."

Asha doubted if her cousin would hire a hitman, even if he could afford to pay him. But Tristan was looking to save face, and she was willing to let him. She nodded. The light turned green. They got moving again.

"But if you serious about this," he said, "the first thing I gotta ask is if you got the money."

Asha nodded. "If it's twenty racks, yeah I do."

"You got that from Larry's house?"

She continued to nod.

It was no secret that Asha was one of few ghetto children who actually inherited something from their parents. Being notified of her father's passing while in prison was one of the darkest moments in her life. They let her out for one day to attend his funeral and then bussed her back to the pen to finish serving her sentence.

Larry never worked a job long enough to qualify for a pension, and he wasn't responsible enough to get life insurance either. But he did pay on his house for over two decades. His daughters were his only heirs. Gloria sold the house and kept Asha's half until she was released. Fresh out of prison with $30,000, everyone thought she would ball out of control and be broke within a year. She surprised them by holding onto as much of it as she could. Two years later, she still had $22,000.

"This should go without saying," Tristan continued, "but if I don't say it, and something happens to you, I'd feel responsible..."

Asha waited for him to speak his piece.

"The man I'ma hook you up with will kill you if you try to short him, or run your mouth, or do anything else to piss him off. I know you been locked up, and you know some killers. Hell, you a killer yo damn self. But this nigga is on another level. He hasn't just killed one or two niggas; it's what he does for a living. He won't have no problem taking you out, if he feel like you done become a problem..."

His words sent a chill down Asha's frame, accompanied by a scattering of goosebumps on her arms. She wasn't sure if it was the warning or the fact that she was so close to getting what she wanted that made her anxious.

Noticing a shift in her energy, Tristan asked, "You still wanna go through with this?"

She nodded.

Tristan's nostrils flared. He sighed and dug a pack of Newport's from his pocket.

"It's alright if I smoke in yo truck?"

It actually was not alright. Since she'd purchased the vehicle, he would be the first person to foul it with cigarette smoke. But she knew he was struggling with her decision, so she shrugged.

"It's fine."

He lit up and offered her the pack. She shook her head.

"You quit smoking again?"

"Yeah."

"You smoked earlier. You mean to tell me this shit we talking about ain't got you needing no square?"

"That cigarette I smoked today was the first one I smoked in nine years. If I smoke another one, I know I'll be right back to smoking them back to back."

Tristan rolled down the window once he got his cigarette lit. He took a long drag and turned towards the window before exhaling.

"What happens now?" Asha asked.

"You can drop me off," he said. "I'll make some calls, and the man will give you a call when he's ready. If you change yo mind before he calls you, make sure you call my ass right away."

"I'm not gon' change my mind," she assured him.

He took another drag before saying, "Yeah, I know you ain't. I knew that soon as you walked up to my car tonight."

Asha knew she'd be treated differently when she returned to work on Monday, but she didn't expect her boss and coworkers to have her in tears within minutes of arriving at Victory Awnings.

In addition to manufacturing custom-made awnings from scratch, the company had three teams that installed them throughout the metroplex. Asha ran into Sharon and Tim, a seamstress and welder respectively, in the shop's parking lot. They both registered surprise and empathy when she pulled up next to them. Sharon wrapped her up in a full body hug when Asha exited her vehicle.

"Hey, girl, how are you? My heart's been bleeding for you."

Tim placed a comforting hand on her shoulder.

"We didn't expect to have you back so soon. How's your family?"

When Asha and Sharon separated, both women had tears in their eyes.

"They're okay," Asha said. "Everybody is just trying to maintain."

"You and your sister are so strong," Sharon said. "I don't think I'd be able to get out of bed, if I was either one of you."

"I feel like that every day," Asha said. "But I can't let depression take hold. I let that happen before, and it wasn't good."

"I've been keeping up with the case on the news," Tim said. "Richey seemed like such a sweet boy. It's a damn shame when you can't even trust your pastor."

Asha's throat caught, and she couldn't respond to that.

Once inside, their boss' smile disappeared when he looked up from his coffee and saw Asha enter the building. Mr. Luck had been walking through the small shop, greeting all of his employees individually, as was his custom. His features were overcome with grief when he and Asha locked eyes. He hurried to her and said, "Asha, what are you doing here?"

"I'm back at work," she said, still trying to recover from the emotions Sharon and Tim had brought to the surface. "Was I supposed to call before I came back?"

"No, no, it's not that. I just... Please, come to my office."

Asha didn't want to follow him, but she knew this talk was unavoidable. She also knew God would use her boss as a vessel to deliver a word that morning.

Coming from generations of money, Mr. Luck retired five years ago after making millions in the awning business. He sold his original company, Luck's Awnings, and became one of Overbrook Meadow's most renown philanthropists. According to Mr. Luck, God called him to do more to help the city's downtrodden, so he started a new business, with the goal of hiring ex-cons and recovered addicts, who often struggled to get a fair shake at life once they overcame their sins. Asha was grateful to have connected with him when she was released from prison.

Inside his office, he turned to her and said, "Asha, you don't have to be here today. I know your nephew's funeral was Friday. I totally understand if you need more time off."

"I appreciate that, Mr. Luck. But I don't want to be at home right now. I feel like I'ma go crazy, if I don't have something meaningful to do."

"But are you okay...?" His blue eyes seemed to cut all the way through her psyche.

Asha's eyes filled with tears once again, and she couldn't lie to him. Unlike most business owners in the *Me too* era, Mr. Luck did not shy away from affection. He stepped to her and hugged her tightly, and then he took hold of her hands. He did not ask if she wanted to pray, because God did not put it on his heart as something optional. Asha closed her eyes, hoping the good word would provide some healing.

When she was first hired, Mr. Luck gave her the option of working in the shop. With the expansion of his business, he needed another seamstress to help Sharon construct and fit the awning canvases to the metal frames once they were crafted by Tim and the other welders. It was Asha's preference to work in the field; installing the awnings at construction sites and established businesses.

Mr. Luck had told her, "I've never had a woman working out of one of the trucks. Are you sure you want that? When it's hot, it's really hot. And when it's cold, it gets *real* cold. Climbing those ladders with an awning in one hand... It's hard work."

"That's fine," Asha had told him. "I been doing hard work for the past seven years. I'm not one of those *girly* girls."

"What were you in for?"

He didn't bat an eye when she told him, "Murder."

"Have you asked God for forgiveness?"

She nodded. "Yes, sir."

"Have you ever worked in construction?"

She shook her head.

"Installed an awning?"

She shook her head again.

"Alright, Asha." He grinned and reached to shake her hand. "You're hired."

Asha considered that encounter when the temperature hit 99 degrees before noon that day. What the hell was she thinking? She could be in the shop with Sharon right now. Her favorite work buddy, Murray, pulled up to a daycare that was still under construction. He parked near the main entrance. The site was bustling with activity. There were workers on the roof and others finishing up projects inside and outside the building.

Asha hopped out of the truck and went to the trailer to retrieve one of the extension ladders. She wore jeans with a tank top and steel-toed boots. Murray tossed her a hardhat before she got too engrossed in her work.

"Hot enough for you?"

Asha cut her eyes at him. "I swear, if you say that shit one more time this summer, I'ma kick yo ass!"

Murray got a laugh out of that. "Yeah right. Queen of the shit-talkers."

"One of these days, I'ma have to make you a believer," she said with a grin.

Murray said something else, but Asha was distracted by her ringtone. She frowned at the unfamiliar number but accepted the call.

"Who's this?"

After a pause, a gruff voice replied, "I'm the man you hired to take care of your problem."

Asha's eyes widened. The intense heat was suddenly not a factor. Her whole body chilled. Her lungs forgot to take their next breath.

"Did you change your mind?" the voice asked.

Asha shook her head, momentarily forgetting that she had to articulate her response. "No," she managed. She considered her boss' prayer that morning, which asked God for healing, peace of mind and forgiveness. "I haven't changed my mind," she said.

"I'm about to give you an address," the caller said. "Don't write it down. Can you be there at seven tonight?"

"Yes," Asha said, although she had no idea where he'd want to meet or how late Mr. Luck would have them out today.

The man gave her an address on a street she'd never been on but in a neighborhood she was familiar with. He then barked more orders. "Don't write that down. If you can't remember it, the deal's off. Don't save this number in your phone and don't be late."

He disconnected, and Asha remembered to breathe. She returned the phone to her pocket with a hand that had gone numb.

Murray, who had been watching her the whole time, assumed the call had something to do with the recent death in her family, and he didn't say a word.

CHAPTER THREE
BOOM

Asha was in a hurry to finish the job at the daycare and install awnings at two more sites before they called it quits that day. Murray didn't question why she was insistent they get back to the shop by six-thirty or why she had remained frazzled after the phone call she received.

Mr. Luck wanted to talk to her again when they returned to the shop, but Asha told him she was headed to her sister's house, and she didn't have time. She knew it was wrong to bring her sister into the lie, but considering what she was about to get involved in, this was a minor transgression.

Thirty minutes later, she pulled into the driveway of a house on the west side of town. The neighborhood was rundown. The house she was parked in front of appeared to be vacant, but Asha noticed the grass had been mowed recently. She sat in her truck for a minute, girding herself for the move she was about to make. With her rap sheet, conspiracy to commit murder could get her as much time as killing someone herself. She considered the hell she'd experienced when she was caged in a concrete zoo for seven long years. She thought about her nephew's smile, and her resolve was strengthened.

She exited the truck and mounted the steps that led to the front porch. Her heart was high in her throat when she reached to knock on the door. The door opened before her knuckles made contact. Asha's eyes moved gradually upward, as she took in the full measure of the man who stood before her. Her lips parted. Her breaths were shallow and unsteady.

The man frowned as he stepped aside to allow her entry. He told her, "Come on."

Asha's knees nearly buckled as she crossed the threshold. The man closed the door behind her and locked it. He turned to face her again, and they spent the next few seconds sizing each other up.

The man was tall, towering more than a foot over her five-foot frame. He wore a thick beard and a ballcap over what appeared to be short hair. His barrel chest protruded through his tee-shirt. His torso was like a tree trunk. His sculpted arms were like huge branches. His eyes were the coldest Asha had ever seen.

She was so overwhelmed by his appearance, she barely noticed there was no furniture in the room, other than an old dining table. The man turned away from her and walked to a stereo that was sitting on the floor in the corner of the room. He knelt and pressed a button on it, and rap music began to play – loudly. Asha noticed the stereo had four wires trailing from it. The wires snaked to each corner of the room. Each wire was connected to a speaker box. With all of them blaring at once, Asha's senses were overwhelmed by the noise.

He approached her again and said, "Come over here," barely loudly enough for her to hear him over the music.

Asha's expression was perplexed as she followed him to the lone table. Sitting atop it was a gadget she didn't recognize. It was roughly the size of a laptop, with two sets of wires extending from it. One end was plugged into the wall. The other was connected to some sort of wand.

He told her, "Empty yo purse and put your cellphone on the table."

Asha could barely hear what he was saying. "What?"

His eyes remained steely as he repeated the instructions.

"Why you got that music so loud?" she nearly shouted.

The look of disapproval that took over his features made her heart stop.

"Don't raise your voice," he said through clenched teeth that were like fangs.

"But I can barely hear you," she reasoned.

"Don't fucking raise your voice," he said again.

Asha didn't think she'd ever been more shook. She placed her cellphone on the table and then her purse. She began to remove the items from it, and he told her, "Just turn it upside down and dump it out."

She had no choice but to comply.

The man reached for his electronic device. He pressed a button on the side, and a small, green light came on. He lifted the wand and slowly passed it over her phone and the contents of her purse. Nothing happened. He made another pass and got the same results. Asha realized he was looking for a wiretap. Her eyes widened as she looked up at him. Outside of a movie, she had never seen anything like this. Who the hell was this man?

He stepped around the table and used the wand to sweep her whole body at the same, mind numbing pace. His closeness made her heart pound even harder. After scanning her front, he told her, "Turn around," and began to scan her back, from head to toe. Finally satisfied, he took a step back and said, "Alright, you can turn back around."

Asha tried to hide her fear as she turned his way again. "Everything cool?" she asked. She knew he hadn't found anything, but she was desperate for his approval.

He placed the wand on the table and nodded. "You can put your stuff back in your purse."

Asha didn't think he'd give her an answer, but as she gathered her things, she asked, "Can you tell me why the music up so loud?"

He told her, "Just because you ain't bugged don't mean you ain't got the laws parked around the corner in a surveillance van."

Once again, Asha had never seen a surveillance van outside of TV. She knew they had high-tech listening devices that could pick up a conversation from blocks away. The fact that this man had a tactic to thwart this let her know that he was the real deal; a professional killer, and he was looking out for her safety as much as he was looking out for himself.

At that moment, she knew she was hiring the right man for the job.

The bearded man with the cold eyes did not lower the volume of the music the whole time Asha was in the house, but they were standing so closely, she didn't have to strain too hard to her what he was saying.

Before she returned her wallet to her purse, he said, "Lemme see your driver's license."

She almost asked him why, but she knew there was no argument she could give that would make him withdraw the request. She handed it to him. He studied it for a few seconds, and she knew he had memorized her personal information – including her address, which was current on the identification card.

He handed it back to her and asked, "You know how much I charge?"

She returned her license to her wallet and looked him in the eyes. "My cousin said twenty thousand."

"That's for a basic job," he confirmed.

He looked her up and down. Her jeans and tank top were soiled from a hard day's work. Her work boots were well-worn.

"You don't look like you got twenty thousand," he decided. "If you don't, I'm prolly gon' leave here and whoop somebody's ass for hooking me up with yo broke ass. What you do for a living?"

Asha tried to hide her offense to his remark. "I work in construction."

"I ain't never heard of no female construction worker. You a dyke?"

"What that got to do with anything?"

"Nothing," he said. "I was just curious."

"I ain't gay."

He didn't comment on that. Instead he said, "I don't know nobody working in construction that got twenty thousand laying around."

"I got the money," she said, no longer hiding her irritation.

"Where you get it?"

"Why?"

"'Cause I asked."

"And I asked you why."

The shift in his eyes made her think he might grab her by the neck if she kept talking back to him.

He told her, "'Cause I need to know if you getting the money from the police."

"I ain't trying to set you up. I don't fuck with the laws."

"Then tell me where you got it from."

Her nostrils flared when she blew out a hot exhalation. Her eyebrows were knitted in frustration when she said, "I got it from my daddy, when he died."

He sneered. "Bullshit. Ain't no nigga ever left nobody nothing when they died."

"We sold his house," Asha said, her features hard, her eyes almost as cold as his. "I wouldn't be here, if I didn't have the money."

He watched her for a few moments and seemed to accept this. His next question was, "Who you want me to get?"

"It's a pastor," Asha said, her expression softening. "His name is Jeremy Butler."

The man's eyes flashed with recognition. "The one who's been on TV for killing that boy?"

Asha nodded. "Yeah, him."

"That ain't no basic job. He got reporters and police all over his ass. I can get him, but it'll cost ten thousand more."

Asha's eyes widened slightly. She shook her head. "I don't have that much."

He continued to study her and asked, "How much you got?"

"Just the twenty. I got twenty-two, if I give you everything I have."

"Why you wanna do that? You saw that shit on TV and felt like somebody needed to take him out? I can't imagine nobody giving up their life savings over something they ain't got nothing to do with."

"I do got something to do with it." She couldn't stop her eyes from watering. She looked away to hide her weakness before saying, "The boy he killed is my nephew."

She watched the man's chest rise and fall.

He told her, "Look me in the eyes."

Asha did, but she hated that he was being so demanding.

"That boy, Richey, that's yo nephew?"

She nodded. "And my godson."

She felt like an eternity passed while he processed this information.

"I'll do it for the twenty," he decided. "Not because I give a shit about your feelings, but because I personally wouldn't mind putting an end to that mess. I think everybody who's heard about that case feels the same way."

Asha's relief was like a cool, spring breeze. Then her frown returned.

"Can you make him suffer?"

"Suffer like what, look him in the eyes and let him know what's about to happen to him – or torture?"

Asha would've preferred both, but he spoke again before she could say so.

"Either way, you can't afford it."

She shook her head, knowing he would say that.

"But if I can get close enough, I'll let him know what's up," the man relented.

Asha wiped the tears from her eyes and told him, "Thank you."

"When you want this taken care of?"

The realization that she was about to have someone killed hit her like a shot of cocaine. The adrenaline rush made her eyes dilate. "As soon as possible."

"When can you get me the money?" he asked. "I need half up front, the other half when I'm done."

"I can have it tomorrow."

"Alright. I'll call you to let you know where to meet me. I'm sure you know I'll come for your ass if you talk to the laws or don't pay me my other half when I'm done. But I'm not gon' kill you first. I'ma kill yo cousin, the one who connected us, and I'ma let you hear about it and simmer on that shit, wondering how long it'll take before I come for you. And when I do come for you, it ain't gon' be no basic job. I'ma look you in the eyes and let you know what's up."

The ominous warning chilled her to the core, even though she had no intentions of not paying or talking to the police.

She told him, "You ain't gotta worry about that."

"After it's done," the man continued, "what you gon' tell the police if they drag you downtown and wanna know where your twenty thousand went?"

"I ain't gon' tell 'em a goddamn thing. I'ma tell them I want a lawyer."

He nodded and then asked, "What if they lock you up?"

"I'ma sit my ass down and be happy with my three hots and a cot. I ain't got no problem doing time for Lil Richey. I ain't gon' say shit."

The bearded man watched her for so long, Asha began to wonder if he had a built-in lie detector.

"Alright," he said at length. "Get yo ass on. I'll call you tomorrow and tell you where to bring that bag."

Asha didn't want to show fear by running from the house, but she gathered her belongings so quickly, it was clear she was not comfortable in the large man's presence.

Her heart rate had not slowed five minutes later when she called her cousin. The freeway would've got her home quicker, but she opted for the side streets. Her mind was already racing fast enough.

Tristan answered after a couple of rings. "What's up?"

"I met that guy," she told him.

"What guy?"

"The one you hooked me up with, to handle that business with the pastor."

"Oh, word? What he look like?"

"You ain't never met him?"

"Hell naw. Don't nobody *wanna* meet that nigga."

"He tall," Asha reported. "Big. Big chest and arms. Got a big ass beard, too."

"He say he gon' do it?"

"Yeah, he finally took the job. Put me through some shit first."

"What you mean?"

Asha told him a little about the encounter.

"Damn. I knew that nigga took his shit seriously, but I didn't know he was doing all that."

"Don't too much scare me," Asha said, "but he had me shook the whole time I was in there. I felt like I was dealing with some international, espionage type of shit. I was expecting some hood nigga."

"He's both," Tristan said. "He real gutter, but he professional too. He been in the game a long time. Everybody know about him, but don't nobody know him. You still gon' go through with it?"

"Yeah. He cut me a deal on the price, 'cause he wants that pastor dead as much as I do. I feel like dealing with him, it won't never get back to me."

"Naw, you ain't gotta worry about that."

Before she got off the phone, Asha asked, "Do you know what his name is?"

"You was talking to him for that long, and you didn't ask the nigga his name?"

"To be honest, I was scared to. I didn't know if he would snap on me, if I did."

Tristan laughed. "It's Boom."

"Boon?"

"Naw, *Boom*, like a shotgun. They say you don't never know that nigga's coming for you. By the time you realize he on yo ass, it's too late. All you hear is **boom**!"

Asha thought the moniker was fitting, and it frightened her all over again. She didn't tell Tristan that Boom had vowed to come for him, if Asha screwed him over in any way. No sense in them both being freaked out.

CHAPTER FOUR
THE JOB

The next morning, Asha debated whether she should show up late to work for the first time in two years or make a trip to the bank during her lunch break. For a $10,000 withdrawal, she knew she'd have to go inside the bank lobby, and they didn't open until eight, which was the same time she was supposed to start her shift. She opted to keep her perfect attendance at Victory Awnings.

Her boss didn't summon her to his office that morning to assess her mental state. He did offer to pair her up with Stephen, who had an easier workload, but Asha said she'd prefer to work with Murray.

"You know that's my road dog," she told him. "Stephen's cool, but between you and me, he takes too many breaks. Me and Murray be trying to get the job done, so we can get to the next site and be done for the day."

Mr. Luck accepted this.

Asha and Murray started their morning with an easy installation at a dentist office before booking it to a strip mall that was in the final stage of construction. That job required a dozen awnings on the storefronts and would take the rest of the day to complete. They could only fit four awnings on their flatbed trailer, so Murray wanted to return to the shop to reload at lunchtime.

Asha didn't have a problem with that, but she told him, "I need to stop by the bank first."

Murray didn't like the idea of bringing their work truck with the extended trailer onto such a small parking lot, but he didn't give her any push back – which was why Asha had chosen to work with him today. Unless she wanted to do something that was so ass-backwards it was unsafe, Murray never complained about the extracurriculars.

"Okay. I'll park at the Kroger's next door."

Withdrawing such a large sum of money took more time than expected, and Asha's jeans weren't baggy enough to conceal the bank envelope in her pocket. She stuffed it in her tool belt before exiting the bank and returned to the truck emptyhanded.

Murray asked her, "What'd you have to do in there?" as he got the truck started.

"Why you in my business?" she asked him.

He shrugged. "Sorry. It's just that you never wanted to stop at the bank before. Didn't mean to get in your business."

"Sorry, I didn't mean to be rude," she said. "I just got a lot going on right now."

He nodded. "I know you do. I been keeping up with the case on the news. You think they gon' find more evidence, so they can arrest that pastor for murder? It's okay, if you don't wanna talk about it."

Asha sighed. She looked over at him and said, "I don't know, man. I don't see how he could do everything he did to my nephew without leaving DNA or *something*. But the police didn't find anything on Richey's body. They didn't find any evidence when they searched the pastor's house, either. They got one of my nephew's fingerprints in his car, but they already knew he was in there from the video. The DA said the kidnapping case ain't even that strong. It might not stick, if they don't find something else."

"If that was my son, I'd probably be in jail right now," Murray revealed. "There's no way I'd be okay with that pervert walking the streets. I'd walk right up to his front door and put a bullet in his head. I'd call the cops myself and wait for 'em to come get me."

Asha nodded but didn't let on how similar their thinking was. When the pastor got what was coming to him, she didn't want anyone to say Asha had a motive and had spoken of revenge. So far Tristan and Boom were the only people who could provide this information, and as far as she was concerned, that was two people too many.

Boom called at two pm. Asha recognized his number, even though she had followed his instructions and didn't have it saved in her phone. The conversation was short and fraught with apprehension.

"Hello?"

He asked, "You got that bag?"

"Yeah," Asha said, her mouth dry.

"I'm finna tell you when to meet me. Don't write it down. If you can't remember it on your own, the deal's off. You ready?"

Asha walked away from the banter of the construction workers in the area before saying, "Okay. I'm ready."

He gave her a location that wasn't an address. He wanted her to meet him on the side of the road, in an underpass. Asha was only vaguely familiar with the area, but she didn't think she'd have a problem finding the spot.

"Can you be there at nine?"

"Yeah."

Asha was glad she didn't have to rush from work this time, but she was not excited about meeting him in an isolated place after sunset. She didn't voice these concerns before Boom abruptly disconnected.

Seven hours later, Asha found the conditions at their meeting place much worse than she had imagined. Not only was the underpass secluded, but the service road that led to it ended abruptly, rather than continue alongside the freeway. If you found yourself on that street, you'd have no choice but to make a U-turn and head in the opposite direction. Asha doubted if anyone would ever find themselves on the deserted road except by mistake.

The underpass itself had no overhead lights to make commuters feel safe after dark. It had become a site for illegal dumping. Asha pulled to a stop under the freeway and looked around warily. Her immediate thought was this looked like a good place to kill someone. She wondered if

Boom had ever lured a poor soul to this very spot for that reason.

She waited for only a few minutes, but it felt like an eternity before a set of headlights turned the corner and pulled to a stop behind her. There had been no traffic in the interim. It didn't seem possible that in a city this populated, there were still a few streets that were relatively deserted. She was not surprised that if such a street did exist, Boom was aware of it.

She rolled down her window and dug the money from her toolbelt as the headlights behind her went dark. The smell of decay quickly filled her truck's cabin and singed her nostrils. She heard a car door open and close behind her. Her sideview mirror revealed a large, hulking figure approaching. Even when he came to a stop next to her, Asha couldn't make out much of his features, only that his beard was as thick as she remembered, and he still wore a ballcap. It was so dark, she couldn't even see the whites of his eyes.

He said, "You got that?"

"Yeah," Asha said, her heart racing. She knew she wasn't on his hit list, but her cousin's words rang in her ear.

*By the time you realize he on yo ass, it's too late. All you hear is **boom**!*

She passed the bank envelope through the window. It disappeared in his large hand.

With a gruff voice, he told her, "I won't be in contact with you again until this is done. You'll probably hear about it on the news, before you hear from me. I won't call you for a few days when I'm finished. I'ma wait to see how much heat it's gonna attract and if any of the heat is on you."

"How, how will you know if the heat's on me?"

"I'll know."

"What, you gon' be following me around or something?"

He ignored the question.

She sighed. "When you gon' do it?"

"It'll be taken care of by Thursday, before midnight."

Today was Tuesday. Asha was happy to know Pastor Butler only had 48 hours to live, but the role she was playing in his demise was nerve-wracking.

She felt like Boom was reading her mind when he said, "I don't ever want you to call me – *unless* you change your mind."

"I'm not gon'–"

"This ain't a time for you to argue with me. I need you to listen."

Asha piped down.

"Do not call me, unless you changed your mind and want to call it off," he repeated. "Don't call me if that man still alive in three days. Don't call me after he dead, if I haven't gotten in touch with you about the rest of the money. If you call me, I'ma shut everything down. I may not answer when you call, but don't take that to mean I didn't get the message. Do you understand me?"

Asha nodded.

"Oh, and if you do call it off, you lose half of your deposit."

"That's fine."

"Alright," he said. "Get gone."

He took a step back to make sure she didn't run over his toes as she fled the scene. He did not return to his vehicle while she watched him in the rearview mirror. It was so dark, Asha couldn't even tell what type of car he was driving.

On Tuesday, Asha tried to carry on with her day as usual, as if someone's life didn't hang in the balance, and she wasn't responsible for whether they lived or died. She knew Boom wouldn't notify her when the deed was done, so she checked the news on her phone obsessively. Lil Richey's disappearance had made the papers throughout the state. His story was propelled to national news when Pastor Butler was arrested.

Asha suspected her nephew's story would begin to trend again when the pastor was found dead. But there were no updates that day. After work, she made two stops before heading home. She had to force herself to eat the burger from McDonald's, but the shots of cognac went down smoothly. She stayed up past midnight before accepting that she may not hear anything until morning.

On Thursday, her previous night's activities caught up with her. She felt like shit, but she didn't give in to her body's urge to vomit or call Mr. Luck and tell him she couldn't make it to work that day.

At lunchtime, Murray asked if she was sick.

Asha didn't feel like she was lying when she said, "I was thinking about my nephew all night. I couldn't sleep."

"It'll get better," he told her. "I know it doesn't feel like it now, but at some point, you'll think about Lil Richey and smile, instead of cry."

Asha didn't think that would ever be the case, but she told him, "Thanks, man. I really hope that's true."

That night, her sister invited her over for dinner. It felt good to be around her family, but there was no denying things were different without Lil Richey there. When Gloria set the table, she left his spot empty, but Richey's sister placed his Paw Patrol placemat in its usual spot. The empty seat was like a dagger in all of their hearts. It crushed Asha's soul, knowing her sister also had to contend with an empty room, a booster seat in her car that was no longer needed, and a multitude of toys that would make her cry every time she came across one.

After dinner, the family moved to the living room. It was Richey's brother's turn to pick a movie. The activity was interrupted by a phone call and then another and then a flurry of them.

The first came to Gloria's cellphone. Her eyes widened as she listened to the voice on the other end. Her mouth fell open at the same pace. Asha's heart began to thunder as she watched her.

Her sister told the caller, "No, I didn't hear anything... Right now...? Okay, I – okay, I'll check it out..."

When she hung up, her husband Richard asked, "What's wrong?"

"It's, um..." Gloria blinked quickly. She scanned the room, her eyes settling on their two children. "Petra says it's something on the news. We need to, um..."

Richard's eyes were as fretful as Asha's.

He said, "What is it, baby?"

"I..." Gloria's eyes moved once again to her children. "Could you take the kids upstairs?"

They immediately protested.

"Why, Mama?" Patrick was seven, going on twenty. "You said I could pick a movie tonight."

"We can do that later," Gloria said. "But it's something on TV we need to watch right now."

"Is it about Richey?" the boy asked.

The tears in Gloria's eyes were all the answer they needed.

"I wanna see," the boy insisted.

Richard did too, but he and his wife were on the same page, when it came to how much drama they wanted to expose their children to.

"Come on," he said, rising from his seat. "Let me and your mom find out what it is first, and we'll talk to you guys about it later."

Despite their anxiety, the kids were obedient. They followed their father out of the room, and Gloria used the remote to find a local news channel.

"Wha, what happened?" Asha asked, with all the innocence she could muster.

"They got more evidence," Gloria said without looking her way. "They think they got enough to arrest the pastor for murder now."

Asha had expected something totally different, but that information still floored her. Her phone rang. Her eyes were glued to the TV while she dug it from her pocket. The Caller ID said it was Tristan's girlfriend Courtney on the other end.

"Hello?" Asha answered.

"Hey, you watching the news?"

"I'm, uh, we trying to find it now."

"They got his ass," Courtney said. "A witness came forward. Girl, I'm so happy right now! They say they might arrest him tomorrow!"

Asha was too numb to react.

"You hear me?" Courtney asked.

"Yeah, lemme... I'll call you back."

The moment she disconnected, her phone rang again. This time it was Uncle Lucius. Gloria's ringtone started to blare as well. Neither of them took another call, until they found the news channel and watched the story themselves.

Channel Six's star reporter, Chad Collins, was excited to inform viewers about a break in Lil Richey's case. The detectives found a witness who saw Pastor Butler's car leaving the area where Lil Richey's body was found. The police had already collected tire tracks from the scene, but they didn't match the pastor's vehicle. Today the detectives found the tires that matched the tracks. They were at a tire shop on the north side of town. The day after Richey's disappearance, Pastor Butler had gone there and replaced all four of his tires with used, rather than new ones.

"These new developments have provided some of the missing pieces," the police chief said at a live press conference. "We've been worried about a lack of physical evidence, and we now understand the extent our suspect has gone to cover his tracks. We believe Pastor Butler bought *used* tires instead of new ones because he knew we'd be suspicious of four new tires if we searched his vehicle.

"With his original tires collected as evidence as well as the statements provided by our witness and the employee of the tire shop, I will speak to the district attorney tomorrow morning and request additional charges be brought against Mr. Butler. These charges will include murder in the first degree, sexual assault, endangering the welfare of a minor, and other related offenses.

"I would like to thank our detectives who have worked tirelessly on this case since the day Richey was reported missing. I know we are far from providing full closure to Gloria and Richard and their family, but we hope these developments will offer them some relief in this unspeakable time. I can take a few questions now..."

Richard had returned to the room by then. All three adults were in tears by the time the press conference ended. Gloria was the first to speak when the news went to commercials.

"Praise God," she said, her hands clasped together, tears streaming down her face.

Her husband took hold of her hand and cradled it in his lap.

"I knew they would get him," Richard said. "I knew God wouldn't let us down. I'ma go check on the kids," he said as he rose from his seat.

When they were alone, Gloria told her sister, "This is what I was talking about at the repast. I told you, you don't have to lift a finger to do God's work."

"I wasn't gonna do anything," Asha told her. "We were just talking, venting."

"I know," Gloria said. "Everyone has that kneejerk reaction – that a killer should immediately be killed."

"That's in the bible," Asha argued. "An eye for an eye."

"But don't you think this is better?" Gloria asked. "That man has never done any time. He'll probably spend the rest of his life in prison. He might even get the death penalty. While he's there, he's gonna experience suffering like you wouldn't believe." She caught herself and offered a weak smile. "Well, I guess you do know what I'm talking about."

Asha knew all too well. Prison was a place of extreme loneliness, fear and anguish. It was complete hell, even for people who were already hardened by the streets. For a clean-cut man like Pastor Butler, each day would be dreadful, especially once the other prisoners found out what he was in for.

"But when you're in prison, at least you're still *alive*," Asha said. "No matter how bad life gets, living is the thing we cherish most."

"I know you don't see it like I do," Gloria replied. "But this is better. Honestly, I would be upset if he commits suicide before they arrest him again. God may not like that I feel this way, but I want him to suffer – every day – for the rest of his life. That's justice to me, and that's justice for Lil Richey."

Halfway across the city, Boom made himself comfortable in the tall branches of a bur oak tree that was one of dozens that lined a dry creek behind his target's property. With the dense foliage and the cover of night, he was completely concealed over twenty feet above the ground. Boom wasn't a fan of tree climbing, but sometimes it came with the job, and when work was concerned, no obstacle was insurmountable.

His target thought he was concealed too. Butler thought the wooden fence that lined his property, coupled with the walls of his home and the ADT security system that may or may not be active kept him safe from anyone who might wish to do him harm. Boom was not deterred by any of this. He wasn't even discouraged by the dozen or so reporters camped out in front of the home, but he did wonder why they were there tonight. They weren't there yesterday when he staked out the property.

Boom assumed there might have been a break in the case, but he didn't check his phone to get the latest news. Though it was dark, and his tree had plenty of leaves, the glow of a cellphone could alert a neighbor who was looking out the window or walking their dog. Boom wondered if the press was there because the police were on their way to re-arrest the pastor. If so, Boom knew his time was running short.

He told Asha he would tell the target why he was about to die if the opportunity presented itself. Boom didn't doubt he could still accomplish that. He could enter the home through the patio door in less than thirty seconds. Butler had an ADT sign in the front yard, but a lot of people kept that sign after their service lapsed. Even if it was active, the response time for a neighborhood like this was at least four minutes. The reporters would hear the alarm, and the pastor would too. Butler may be armed, but Boom had a flashbang that would disorient his target. He could end the pastor's life and make his getaway in less than one minute.

But Asha didn't pay him enough for that, and it would be much simpler to take care of this from the tree. At that moment, Pastor Butler sat at a computer desk in his bedroom. He had made a few trips to the front of the house to check on the reporters before returning to the desk. His curtains were drawn. The average observer couldn't have tracked his movements, even if there was no fence, but Boom was six feet above the fence, and the infrared scope on his sniper rifle saw everything. His weapon was military grade. With it, Boom could see through walls, but his target made things easier by positioning himself in front of a window.

At this distance, a headshot would be as easy as tossing a coin into a fountain. Boom cocked his weapon. The sound of his gun chambering a round was the most noise he'd made since arriving at the location.

His finger moved to the trigger. He held his breath.

And then his phone vibrated in his pocket.

He waited, and it vibrated again and then again. Finally, the call was sent to a voicemail he hadn't set up.

Boom did not have to check his phone to know who had called him. Only one person had the number to this throwaway, and he had instructed her not to contact him unless she wanted to call it off.

Boom felt no irritation as he checked his weapon and began to dismantle it, before returning it to his backpack. Asha had just paid him $5,000 to climb a tree. He wasn't mad at her at all.

CHAPTER FIVE
COMPROMISED

Asha fretted for the rest of the night, wondering if Boom had received her call and interpreted it correctly. He told her he may not answer, but if she called, he would shut everything down. Asha had never known anyone to operate like that. What harm would there have been in texting her "Okay," or a simple thumbs up emoji? Without confirmation, she didn't get much sleep that night.

But in the morning, there was no breaking news announcing the pastor had been murdered. At noon that day, Gloria called while she was at work.

"Hey," Asha answered.

"Did you hear?" her sister asked.

Asha still suspected Boom had killed the man, but she hoped for the best. With her stomach bubbling, she said, "Naw, I haven't heard anything. What's up?"

"They just arrested him," Gloria breathed.

Asha brought a hand to her face and blew out a sigh of relief.

"They had cameras outside his house when his lawyer showed up and took him to turn himself in," Gloria continued. "They wouldn't answer any questions, but seeing the look in that bastard's eyes when he walked out of his house..." She sighed. "That man knows his life is over. He looked so pitiful, and it made my heart feel so *good*. A lawyer called me this morning. I don't know how she got my number, but she said after the pastor is convicted, I can sue him for everything he has. I can get his house, his savings and whatever other assets he got. She said I can sue the church too, but I don't think I wanna go that far."

"Really? That's good, Sis. You need to break his ass for everything."

"It'll take a while before all of this goes through the courts, but she wanted to be the one to represent me when it's time. She tried to get me to come to her office to sign a retainer–"

"Nah, if she trying to get you this bad, it's because she's thinking about her cut. You need to wait it out and go with a lawyer who'll take the less money out of whatever you got coming."

"I know. That's what Richard said too."

"I'm glad things are going better for you," Asha said. "None of this is gonna make the pain go away, but having his ass back in jail is a start."

"Yeah, it is. What about you?"

"What you mean?"

"Have you thought about what we talked about? Do you think this is better than him being dead?"

If I wanted him dead, he'd be dead right now, Asha thought. She said, "Yeah, it is. You were right. It is better this way."

Asha tried to get immersed in her work after the call, but her thoughts were all over the place. Boom didn't make things any better when he called her at two o'clock.

Asha accepted the call and dipped into a restroom on the construction site. The mirror over the sink revealed a look of dread she always seemed to wear when she had interactions with this man.

"Hey," she said in a hushed voice.

He said, "Can you meet me tonight, at the same house we met at the first time?"

"I called you last night," she said. "I know you said you wouldn't answer, but—"

"Can you be there at eight o'clock?"

The hairs stood on the back of her neck.

"Yeah. That's cool. I wanted to tell you what happened, why I had to call you. I know I said—"

He cut her off. "*Stop talking.* I don't move like that on no phone. Just meet me tonight, so we can settle up."

He hung up on her.

Asha continued to stare at her reflection, frozen in place with her phone next to her ear. Her look of dread had transitioned to terror. She still had at least three more hours to work today. She didn't think she could make it to quitting time without having a nervous breakdown. But an hour later, work served as a suitable and necessary distraction.

By the time she and Murray returned the company truck to the shop, all Asha could think about was the dark, bearded man.

There was only one person in her life she could talk to about this particular problem, so she called Tristan when she got on the freeway.

"Yo," he answered. "What up, cuzzo?"

Asha was too flustered to ease into the conversation. "Say, I think that nigga gon' kill me."

"What? What you talking about?"

"Boom. He want me to meet him tonight."

"Wait, hold up. Let me go over here..." She heard movement on the phone. After a few moments, he said, "Why you say something like that? Something went wrong? I know he didn't kill that dude, 'cause I saw him on the news getting arrested."

"I told him not to," Asha reported. "I called it off last night."

"Why you do that?"

"'Cause I was at G's house, and they were talking about arresting him again today. G was so happy, and she was talking about how this was better than him getting killed."

"*You told her you was finna get that nigga killed?*" Tristan had gone from zero to a hundred.

"*No.* She said him being in prison was better than him committing suicide – just dying in general."

"So, you called and told Boom not to do it."

"Yeah."

"Damn, Asha, I told you this wasn't nothing to play with."

"I know, but when I saw him a couple of days ago, he made it sound like it was okay if I called it off."

"Oh. Then what you trippin' on?"

"He wants to meet me tonight. He said he wants to settle our business."

"He gon' give your money back?"

"Not all of it. He said he'd keep five G's, if I backed out."

"You – I don't see what you worried about. He said he wants to settle your business, and he owes you five G's. You don't think that's why he wants to meet you?"

"I don't know," Asha said. "I got a bad feeling about it."

"He sounded mad or something?"

"He *always* sound mad. I think since he didn't do the job for me, he done exposed himself to somebody he don't got no leverage on."

"That ain't no reason to take you out."

"I ain't so sure about that."

"I think you wrong," Tristan said. "But if you really feel that way, don't go. Let him keep that little change."

Five thousand dollars was not *a little change*, but that was beside the point.

"He knows where I live," Asha said. "If I don't go, he gon' *really* wanna kill me. He'll probably think I'ma tell on him."

"What you want me to do?" Tristan asked. "You want me to show up to wherever y'all meeting and keep an eye on you?"

"Unless you come in the house with me, you can't keep an eye on me."

"I can show up before you get there and get that nigga first."

Despite her whirlwind of emotions, Asha almost laughed at that. Tristan would have a better chance killing a grizzly bear with his bare hands.

"No, I don't want nothing like that. I just – hell, I don't know what I want. I guess I just wanted to tell somebody, in case something happens to me."

"What time you meeting him?"

"Eight o'clock."

"Gimme the address."

"Why?"

"In case you don't call me later, at least I'll know where to start looking."

Asha knew that wasn't a good idea. If Boom wasn't upset with her now, he'd kill her for sure if he knew she gave the address to someone. But as tough as she appeared to others, Asha knew she was a 140-pound female going to meet a bona fide killer who was almost twice her size. It would be foolish not to have *some* kind of backup.

She gave Tristan the address.

Asha's warning signs were blaring as she mounted the steps of Boom's meeting spot on the west side of town. As was the case the last time she visited this house, the door swung open before she had time to knock. She stepped inside and encountered the only man she had ever known who made her heart squeeze uncomfortably, at the mere sight of him.

Boom wore dark pants with a dark tee and his customary ball cap. He didn't appear to have any weapons on him, but that didn't ease Asha's tension. A man of his caliber was sure to have a pistol concealed *somewhere*, probably tucked in the small of his back or in an ankle holster.

The front room was still barren, with the exception of the lone table and the stereo in the corner. Asha waited for him to turn the music on like he did last time, but he walked to the table and turned to face her. Without the music, Asha wasn't forced to stand close to the brooding beast, so she maintained a respectable six feet between them.

Boom reached towards his back, and she couldn't stop herself from flinching. But he retrieved a stack of money, rather than a weapon. He placed it on the table, watching her oddly.

"Why you so jumpy?"

She shrugged. "I don't know. You make me nervous."

"What you got to be nervous about?" he asked. "Have you done something I wouldn't be happy about?"

Asha thought about Tristan as she shook her head. She maintained eye contact, because this man always seemed to be filtering lies from the truth.

"I thought you'd be mad because I called it off yesterday," she offered.

He watched her for a few seconds before saying, "I told you I'd keep half the deposit if you changed your mind. I didn't say it would be a problem."

"I know, but the way you were talking to me on the phone..."

He shrugged. "I don't talk business over the phone. You sounded like you were gonna keep talking, so I hung up. I figured anything you had to tell me, you could say it in person."

Asha thought that was the closest he'd ever come to apologizing for being so freaking rude.

"Do you wanna know why I changed my mind?" she asked him.

He said, "I already know. I checked the news after you called me. Since the man was going to jail, you probably think that's good enough, no need to kill him."

"You were okay with that?"

"Yeah. It was your job. Why would I care?"

"You said you wanted him dead too."

"I know a lot of people that I would prefer were not breathing. But I don't just go around taking people out. Just like you probably drive around and see a lot of businesses that need an awning, but you don't go home and make one."

Asha's eyes widened. "How do you know what I do for a living?"

"It's okay for you to know what I do, but I can't know what you do?" he asked.

That was not an answer to her question, but Asha knew it was all he'd give her.

He surprised her by saying, "To be honest, I think most of the people I kill is a dumb move."

She frowned. "Then why do you do it?"

"It's what I do for a living. But for the people who hire me, I don't think they understand that when you kill a man, that's it. They can't pay you what they owe, they not scared no more. They don't suffer. One minute they eating a fucking steak, and the next second their brains are on the plate. In the blink of an eye, all their worries and responsibilities are gone. Death sends a message – I can't argue with that. But I think it lets the dead guy off too easy. As far as that pastor, prison is a better alternative."

Asha couldn't believe he was being so insightful and open. It was like she was talking to a regular person, rather than the boogeyman. Since they were being cordial, she asked, "Why don't you have the music on today?"

"Because I did my research," he said. "I know you're that boy's aunt. Your reason for hiring me checked out. I trust you."

Asha didn't think Boom would ever say anything to make her feel genuinely happy, but it felt good to hear him say that.

"Take your money," he said. "I gotta bounce. Got some things to do tonight."

Asha stepped closer to him and collected the stack of bills. When they were within touching distance, she felt a pulse of energy radiating from him. Her pulse quickened, for a different reason this time.

"Thank you," she said as she backed away. She knew this was the last time she'd see him and felt she should offer more meaningful parting words, but she couldn't think of any.

He watched her as she turned and walked to the door.

And then he charged forward and grabbed hold of her.

Asha's scream got caught in her throat as he wrapped his large arms around her and they crashed to the floor. He said something, but Asha's brain didn't catch up to his words before she heard gunshots.

What he had said was, *"**Get down**!"*

A second later a barrage of gunfire ventilated the door she'd been standing in front of.

PAP! PAP! PAP-PAP-PAP-PAP!

In a split second, Asha's survival instincts kicked in. She realized that as implausible as it was, they were being shot at, and Boom had just saved her life. He used the lull in the shooting to bark more orders.

"Come on. Get moving. We gotta go."

His voice was almost conversational, so much so, Asha stared at him in disbelief, wondering if this was real. He began to drag her in the desired direction, when she didn't get moving quickly enough.

Shots rang out again, this time through the front window. Asha winced as glass rained on them and bullets whizzed overhead. She tried to resist the urge to panic as she scrambled for cover, but it was hard not to. The realization that someone was trying to kill them didn't vibe with anything she knew about Boom. According to Tristan, everyone on the streets was afraid of him. Who would have the gall to–

Tristan.

No. He, of all people, wouldn't do something this stupid. Whoever was gunning for them was doing so indiscriminately. If it was her cousin, he could've killed her with this sloppy attempt to save her life.

"Come on!"

Boom was still urging her forward, but he was no longer babying her. Through squinted eyes, Asha saw that he had made it all the way to the kitchen, still crawling on all fours. He reached up for the door leading into the garage and then disappeared through it.

She hurried to catch up, her eyes wide, broken glass grinding into her knees as she scurried after him. She made it to the garage and saw Boom climb behind the wheel of a mean, black SUV that was backed into the spot. She hurried to the passenger side and got in beside him. He started the truck and was still astonishingly calm when he looked over and asked her, "What side did you park on?"

"*What's happening?*" Asha squealed. "*What the fuck is going on?*"

"Did you park on this side of the garage, or are you on that side?"

Boom pointed to the spot in front of them and then to the right.

Asha realized what he was getting at and racked her brain for the answer. "I'm on the left side," she said, "over there."

"Good," he said. "You might wanna buckle up."

Asha remained frozen, her eyes wide and unblinking. Boom did not give her time to come to her senses. He gunned it. The squeal of his tires was deafening in the small garage, but that was nothing compared to the sound of his SUV crashing into the closed garage door.

WHAM!

The jolt of the impact nearly tossed Asha from her seat. She thought he had gone crazy, but Boom's calculation was correct. One of the inanimate objects had to yield, and the SUV won.

71

The bottom of the garage door was torn from its hinges. It scraped the top of the SUV from the hood to the back of the roof before the whole door fell behind them with another loud **BANG!** The truck's front windshield looked like someone had taken a bat to it, but it held firm. Boom could see well enough through the cracks to make a quick right turn and speed down the darkened street.

A volley of gunshots followed them. Asha cowered as they impacted the SUV.

TINK! TINK! TINK-TINK!

She sank low in her seat with her arms over her face.

Boom made another right at the next corner. His tires squealed again as he stomped the gas pedal.

"*What the fuck?*" Asha cried. "*What the hell is happening?*"

"Did you tell somebody where you was going tonight?" Boom checked the rearview mirror before making a left and headed towards the freeway.

"*No! I already told you that!*" Asha prayed Tristan didn't have anything to do with this. She sat up tentatively and looked back to see if anyone was following them. There were no headlights headed in their direction. Whoever had ambushed them was not in hot pursuit. Boom must have felt this way too, because he was no longer driving at breakneck speeds.

He asked her, "Did you leave anything in your truck?"

"*What?*" She looked over at him, her eyes frantic.

"You left your truck at that house," he said. "Whoever shot at us has access to it. Do you have anything in it?"

She shook her head, her face set in a scowl. "No. Just some tools and stuff."

72

"Are you sure there's nothing in it with your name on it? You got an insurance card in the glove box, anything like that...?"

Asha's breath caught. "Yeah, my insurance card is in there. And, and my purse. I left my purse in the truck."

CHAPTER SIX
ASSHOLE

Five minutes later, they were on the freeway traveling the speed limit.

Boom muttered, mostly to himself. "I need to hurry up and get this car off the road. We riding round looking like a hit and run."

Asha agreed with that assessment. By then, she was more inquisitive than afraid. She knew Boom was on the same page.

"I need you to think real hard," he told her. "Is there anyone who would've followed you to that house?"

She shook her head. "No. Why would somebody be following me?"

"You ain't pissed nobody off lately?"

"Pissed them off to the point where they wanna kill me? No. There's nobody in my life that would do something like that. I don't do nothing but go to work and kick it with my family. I ain't into nothing dangerous."

"Are you sure? Maybe there was a misunderstanding that didn't seem like a big deal. You never know how far people will take something."

She frowned at him. "Why you think I had something to do with this? What about you? Is it somebody in *your* life that wants to kill you?"

She was surprised to see him grin at that. "Yeah. Probably a couple dozen people."

Her eyes widened. "Are you serious?"

"Yeah, if not more. I done bodied a lot of people. Wouldn't surprise me if somebody try to avenge one of 'em."

"Then why you charging me up, if you know you got that many enemies?"

"Because tracking down one or two enemies on your end would be a helluva lot easier than figuring out who it is on my end. I didn't wanna go through that, if you had some idea who it was."

"This doesn't have anything to do with me," Asha assured him.

"It's cool," he said. "I'ma figure it out. There may be a lot of people who want me dead, but not too many of them can get that close. It really don't make sense," he mused. "Whoever it is gotta be *somewhat* legit, or they never would've tracked me down. But then they turn around and shoot up the house like a goddamn gangbanger. That's why I thought they were gunning for you. They waited for you to walk up to the door."

"Or maybe they thought it was *you* walking up to the door. How'd you even know they were there?"

"I heard something," he said. "Thought it sounded like somebody cocking a gun. I wasn't sure, but I didn't wanna take no chances. When you walking up to a door, and you hear a gun cock on the other side, I know what that shit means. I used to get down like that, before I started charging people for a hit. I learned real quick that you don't never

75

know if you got 'em unless you see it with your own eyes. Whoever pulled this shit finna learn too. Think they can take me out with some pussy shit? They gon' learn the hard way."

His words were so cold, they gave Asha chills. She told him, "Thank you."

"For what?"

She thought it was obvious. "For saving my life."

He grunted. "Now that's something I don't hardly ever hear. Might be the first time."

Asha frowned at him as he exited the freeway. Did this man not have one courteous bone in his body? She was about to ask him if he'd ever heard of the words, *You're welcome,*" when her cellphone rang. Her heart froze when she pulled it from her pocket and saw that it was Tristan calling. She almost didn't answer, but she feared he'd go to the address she'd given him, if she didn't let him know she was alright. The shooter was probably long gone, but the police might be there. She could imagine Tristan's reaction if he saw her truck parked at an active crime scene.

She told Boom, "I gotta take this call."

He stopped at a light and looked her in the eyes. "Okay, but be careful what you say."

Asha tried to suppress her apprehension. She knew this had to be the performance of her life. She prayed her fingers didn't tremble as she accepted the call and brought the phone to her ear.

"Hey, what's up?"

"What's up with you?" Tristan asked. "You good?"

"Yeah, I'm good."

"You and Boom handled y'all business? Wasn't no problems?"

Asha was relieved to hear that her cousin had nothing to do with the shooting, but Boom was staring right at her. The look in his eyes made Asha wonder if he could hear Tristan's end of the conversation.

"Yeah, it's all good," she told her cousin. "What you getting into tonight?"

"I'm on the block. You wanna swing through?"

"Naw, I had a long day. Finna take my ass to bed."

"Alright. I'm sorry you had to give up five G's, but I know you glad that shit's over..."

"Yeah, I am. I'll holler at you later."

Boom continued to watch her as she disconnected. The traffic light finally turned green. As they passed through the intersection, Asha cursed the signal light for conspiring against her.

"Why you so nervous?" he asked, his eyes back on the road. "I don't like to be around nervous people. You never know what they up to."

There was no point in denying the obvious, so she told him, "I'm nervous because we just got shot at. Now I'm in the car with you, and I don't know where we going, and I got people calling, and I don't know what to tell them. You was looking at me like if I said one wrong thing, you'd slap the shit outta me. Why *wouldn't* I be nervous? Where the hell you taking me anyway?"

He studied her eyes before responding. "Where you want me to take you? You wanna go home?"

"I thought you said they probably got my address. You don't think they'll come looking for me?"

Boom shrugged. "Maybe. If they think you're somebody I care about, or somebody they can snatch to find out where I'm at, they probably will."

Asha cocked her head as she stared at him. "And you're okay with me getting *snatched* over some shit I ain't got nothing to do with?"

"I didn't say that. I asked if you *wanted* to go home. I didn't say it was a good idea."

"But you would let me do it, if I told you to take me home?"

He rolled his eyes. "I ain't no kidnapper."

Her expression was incredulous. "No, what you are is an *asshole*."

He fixed a mean glare on her. She didn't back down.

She told him, "I don't care if you kill me. I mean, I do care, but until that day comes, you need to work on your communication skills. Would it kill you to act like you *might* have a heart?"

He cracked a smile and shook his head. "Okay, so you don't wanna go home. Want me to drop you off somewhere, with a friend or somebody in your family?"

"I don't know. Why don't you tell me if *you* think that's a good idea?"

"Probably not," he said. "Depending on who's coming for me and how professional they are, they might track you down. You could bring trouble to somebody you care about."

"Then why would you suggest it, if you know it ain't a good idea?" She was nearly exasperated. "Do you have another plan that doesn't involve throwing me to the wolves?"

"I got a place where you can lay low for a day or two, until I figure out who shot at us and whether they're even interested in you."

"Okay. Where is this place?"

Boom turned on a quiet street in an east side neighborhood. He told her, "It's right up here on the left."

She eyed him curiously. "So you were taking me there all along...?"

He nodded. "Even though I'm an *asshole*, I wouldn't throw yo ass to the wolves."

Asha was appreciative, but she didn't know what to make of him. She told him, "Thank you."

He surprised her again with his response. "You're welcome."

Boom backed his battered SUV into a three-car garage. There were two other vehicles parked there; a black Charger and another Suburban that was identical to the one he was driving. They exited the vehicle and entered a house that was completely different than the one they met at an hour ago. It was clear someone lived here.

The kitchen was neat and spacious. The open floor plan revealed a living room that was equally neat and fully furnished. The style was modest, and there were a few touches that made Asha wonder if a woman lived there. Boom didn't strike her as someone who would devote a lot of time to the intricacies of home décor.

He led her through the house, down a hallway, and stopped at one of the bedroom doors. He pushed it open and stepped aside.

He told her, "You can sleep here."

Asha peered into the room before stepping inside. The room had a queen-size bed, a dresser and a nightstand. There was a 52-inch TV mounted on the wall. The bed was made, and she didn't see anyone's personal effects lying around.

He said, "Go ahead and make yourself comfortable. I gotta make a few calls before I take off. You hungry? I can make you something to eat."

Asha didn't know how she could make herself comfortable without any of her belongings. She asked him, "Where you going?"

"Talk to a few people," he said. "See if the streets know anything about what happened tonight."

Asha thought she might watch a little TV later, but the most important electronic she needed was her phone. "Do you have an iPhone charger?" she asked.

He nodded. "I'll bring you one before I leave," he said, before continuing down the hallway.

Forty minutes later, Asha was lured from her room by the smell of food. She wasn't hungry when she arrived at the house, but her stomach started to growl when she walked to the kitchen and saw Boom standing at the stove. He had changed into jeans and a dark blue tee. The shirt stretched over the muscles in his chest and arms. Water boiled in one pot, while he browned ground beef on another burner.

But the biggest surprise was his face, which was now clean-shaven. Asha stepped closer, her eyebrows knitting together as she stared at him. He turned towards her. Without his ball cap, she saw that his hair was short, styled in a crew cut. With the beard gone, she felt like she could see his lips for the first time. His jawline was hard and rigid. Even though beards had become the go-to style for masculinity, Asha thought he was just as rugged without it. She didn't think she blinked for a full thirty seconds. It was as if she was seeing him for the first time.

"You ready to eat?" he asked.

She nodded. "You shaved your beard?"

That was an obvious question, so he didn't bother answering.

He told her, "I'm making spaghetti. I'm almost done."

"Okay."

"I left a charger over there," he said, gesturing towards the kitchen table. "You can eat there when I finish."

She moved in that direction, but her eyes remained glued on him.

"What you looking at?" he asked.

She shook her head as she took a seat. "You look so diffcrent."

"In my line of work, it doesn't pay to look the same every time."

She continued to watch him as he finished cooking the meat and then drained the noodles. He went to a well-stocked pantry and came out with a jar of Ragu.

"I normally wouldn't use this stuff," he told her, "but I don't have time to make it from scratch."

"It's fine."

He returned to the stove and finished cooking their dinner. Asha noticed that he took several seasonings from the cabinet to add to the sauce. He used a fork to taste a mouthful of spaghetti before deciding it was to his liking. He moved again to get a plate. He prepared a serving and brought the still smoking meal to the table and placed it before her.

"You not eating with me?" she asked.

"No. I'll probably pick up something. I'm 'bout to go."

"Where are you going? I really don't want to be left here alone – after what happened."

"You're safe here," he assured her.

"We weren't safe at that other house."

She could tell he wanted to go, but he remained there long enough to entertain her for a minute.

"This house is different," he said.

"Do you live here?"

"You asking too many questions."

"This place is really big, for one person. I was just wondering if there was a woman living here with you," she said, thinking about some of the decorations in the living room. "I don't wanna be surprised if someone walks up in here."

"No one is walking up in here," he said with a grin. "This is where I lay my head most of the time, and when I do, I'm alone."

She sighed.

He remained standing next to the table. "You not hungry anymore?"

"Yeah, I am. I just... I'm not sure what I'm supposed to do while you're gone."

"You never laid low before?"

"Yeah, but not in a house I'd never been to."

"If I'm willing to leave a stranger here by herself, you should be okay with it too."

"How long do you think I'll have to stay?"

He shrugged. "I don't know. I wanna take care of this as soon as possible. I gotta shut everything down, until I find out who's after me. I can't make no money like that."

"I was asking because I don't have any clothes. Am I supposed to sleep in these jeans and wake up in 'em too? I don't even want to get in that clean bed wearing my work clothes."

"You could bathe and sleep naked."

She shot him a look and he smiled.

"Alright. Gimme your sizes, and I'll pick some stuff up for you."

She thought he was going to tell her he already had women's clothes there. She was happy with the alternative. She gave him her sizes. She wasn't surprised that he didn't write it down.

"Is that it?" he asked. "You need anything else?"

"No, I guess not."

"I know you got some people you wanna call," he said. "Don't tell them where you at or who you're with. I don't care what kind of story you have to come up with, but my name bet not be in it."

"You never even told me your name."

"I thought you got it from your cousin. It's Boom."

"Why they call you that?" She already had Tristan's version of the story, but she was interested in hearing his side of it.

"A shotgun used to be my weapon of choice," he revealed. "I was surgical with that shit. When my targets saw me coming, *boom* was the last thing they'd ever hear."

The explanation was just as chilling as when Tristan told her.

"You don't use a shotgun anymore?" she asked.

He shook his head. "Nah. Most of my targets never see me at all. Why I wanna get within twenty feet, when I can accomplish my mission from fifty yards away?"

Fifty yards? Jeez. Asha felt like she'd forever be awed by this man.

"Alright, I'm out," he said. He left the table and headed for the door leading to the garage. He turned back and said, "I was serious about bathing and sleeping naked if you want to. It's after nine. I don't know when I'll be back. I don't want you sitting there fonky and tired, waiting on me to bring you something to wear."

She frowned and looked down at her shirt. "I'm *fonky*?"

"Naw, but you worked construction all day on one of the hottest days of the year. You know you don't smell like Bath and Body Works right about now."

Her mouth fell open.

Fucking asshole.

She wished she had voiced that thought aloud before he exited the kitchen and was gone. She also kicked herself for not insisting that he at least give her one of his tee shirts. Even if it was too big, it was better than being naked in a stranger's house.

CHAPTER SEVEN
UNINTENDED CONSEQUENCE

Asha waited for as long as she could, but Boom's spaghetti gave her the itis, and her body felt drained as her adrenaline rush subsided. At midnight, she stepped into the shower connected to the bedroom he'd directed her to. Her senses were on high alert as the hot spray soothed her weary muscles. She had always felt people were at their most vulnerable when they bathed. An intruder could use the sound of water as cover and make it all the way to the bathroom, catching you naked and defenseless.

She turned the water off ten minutes later and listened intently to the sounds in the house. Thankfully there were none – and then, all of a sudden, there was.

Asha grabbed a towel to cover herself as she craned her ear in the direction of the faint hum of a mechanical device. Initially she wasn't sure what it was. She let out a sigh when she realized it was the garage door opening. Boom had returned.

Or had he?

He seemed confident that this house was safe from the person who was out to get him, but how could he be sure? If they could find him at the first house, why not here?

Asha wrapped the towel around her torso and tucked the corner between her breasts, so she'd have full use of both hands. She scurried to the kitchen and found a cutlery set on the counter. She selected the largest knife and ducked around the corner next to the garage door just as someone twisted the knob. A large, dark figure entered the kitchen. Asha lie in wait behind him. She could tell by his outfit that it was Boom, but by then she had worked herself into an irrational panic. She wouldn't know for sure until she saw his face.

Sensing someone behind him, he turned and eyed her queerly. Asha blew out another sigh as she lowered the knife. He continued walking casually into the kitchen. He deposited several plastic bags on the counter before facing her again.

"What the hell are you doing?" he asked.

"Protecting myself from whoever was coming in the house," she replied. She walked past him and returned her weapon to the knife block. "I don't like you leaving me here with no protection," she told him, her eyes set in a frown. "It's bad enough I don't feel comfortable here. What am I supposed to do if somebody breaks in while you're gone?"

"I told you nobody was gonna come here."

"But you haven't told me why you so sure about that. You didn't think anybody would find that other house."

He rolled his eyes. "What kind of protection you want, Asha? A strap?"

She nodded. "Yeah. I know you got plenty of 'em."

"Did you have a gun in your purse or in your truck?"

She shook her head.

He told her "I don't think you should have one now, if you didn't have one before."

"I used to keep a pistol on me," she informed him. "But I haven't had one since I got out the pen. I wasn't trying to do nothing to get me locked up again."

He looked her up and down. He stared so long, Asha began to feel self-conscious. With the towel draped around her longways, her bare legs were fully revealed. The fabric only extended a couple of inches past her box. Her hands subconsciously came together between her legs, but it was her arm Boom was looking at.

He told her, "Lemme see that tat."

She showed him her arm. The tattoo featured a clock with the time immortalized at seven o'clock. A few chains were draped over the timepiece. The artwork was detailed, with expert shading and a few cracks on the clock's face.

"That looks too good to be done in prison," Boom noticed.

"I got it a few days after I got out," she confirmed.

"Lemme guess, the clock and the chains represent time wasted while you were behind bars. The seven is how many years you did."

Asha nodded, her eyes reflective. "You the first person to get that right on the first try."

"What were you in for?"

The coldness in her eyes returned. "Murder."

"You got ten for that and did seven?"

She nodded again. "The judge gave me a little pity because I had some extenuating circumstances."

"Alright," Boom decided. "I'll give you a pistol, if I have to leave you here again."

"Thank you." She looked over at the bags he'd brought with him but didn't inquire about them. Instead she asked, "Did you find out anything?"

"Yeah," he said. "But not much. Somebody put a hit out on me, and somebody was stupid enough to take the job. I gotta body everybody involved, before this is all said and done. But right now, I don't know shit. I'll try again tomorrow."

He looked her up and down again. "You decided to bathe."

"Yeah, because I'm *fonky*, remember?"

He chuckled. "You don't take too much shit, do you?"

"I didn't use to, but I feel like I been taking a lot of it, since I met you."

He shook his head. "Damn, woman. You don't let up." He reached for the bags and handed them to her. "Here. I hope you not into designer shit, because Walmart is the only thing open 24 hours."

Asha took them and said, "No, it's cool. Thanks."

He took in her physique one more time before saying, "I woulda bought you a dress, if I knew you had legs like that."

"I don't wear dresses."

"How I know you'd say that?" he replied before walking away.

In her room, Asha looked through the things he'd brought her. There were three pairs of jeans, three tee shirts, three sets of undergarments, a pair of sneakers and a package of socks. As far as toiletries, he provided her with a comb, brush, toothbrush, toothpaste and a tube of deodorant. Asha wondered if he didn't know she'd need products for her hair or didn't consider it a necessity.

She also noticed that he hadn't included any sleepwear. First, he suggested she sleep nude. Now, he assumed she'd be okay in a bra and panties. She assumed this was an oversight, rather than a sneaky attempt to get a glimpse of her body, so she didn't plan on mentioning it.

The next morning, she awakened at 7 o'clock, fifteen minutes after her alarm would've sounded if she was home. With everything going on, she shouldn't have been too bothered about calling-in to work, but she was. Her boss was a good man who had gone out of his way to help the city's unemployable. She always felt the least she could do was show up every day.

But Mr. Luck was understanding.

"It's okay, Asha. I already said you should take more time off to spend with your family. I'll take you off the schedule today and all of next week."

"Thank you, but I don't need that much time."

"Well, go to the movies or take a road trip. You need some family time and some you time, Asha. I'm serious about this, and I won't take no for an answer."

"Okay, Mr. Luck. Thank you."

She crawled out of bed and dressed in one of her new outfits. She styled her hair as best she could with just a comb and a brush. She exited the room and saw that Boom had not yet stirred. That gave her an opportunity to explore his kitchen and prepare breakfast for her caretaker. Boom didn't have bacon or sausage, but he had enough eggs, veggies and shredded cheese to put together a nice omelet. She paired the meal with toast and coffee.

It was her good cooking that lured the man of the house this time, but by the looks of it, he had already been up for some time. Asha's eyes bugged out of her head when she saw the new Boom, which had somehow returned to the *old* Boom.

"*What the fuck is going on?*" she breathed as she left the stove and walked up to him.

His beard was back in full flair, as thick as it was the last time.

He shook his head, grinning.

"You did not grow that thing back overnight," she said, shaking her head. "Wait, is that... *Is that real?*"

He continued to shake his head.

"But, it, it..." She reached up and stopped herself. "Can I touch it?"

"Yeah. You can touch it and pull on it, but not too hard."

Asha examined the beard with fingers that were as disbelieving as her eyes. She stood on her toes to stare at it more closely. Due to the beard's thickness, she couldn't tell where or how it had been affixed to his face.

"This is amazing," she said as she backed away.

"Funny to hear a woman say that," he replied. "Y'all can go from baldheaded to hair down to your ass in a couple of minutes."

"Yeah, but I've never seen it done like this – with a beard. What are you, some kind of master of disguise?"

"I told you, in my line of work, it don't pay to look the same every time. Everybody knows Boom for his beard. When they see that beard coming, they know what time it is. But sometimes, I don't want them to know what time it is."

She nodded, still awed by the extent in which he'd concealed his identity.

"You made omelets?" he asked, looking at the plates on the counter.

"Oh – yeah. I would've put some meat in them, but you don't have any."

"I can stop and get some later. I gotta make a couple of moves, and then I'll check to see if your apartment is safe."

"You wanna take me home?"

"Yeah, if it's safe. Don't you wanna go?"

Asha frowned, not sure what she wanted anymore. She asked him, "Can I go with you when you leave?"

"I prefer to work alone. But I know you don't wanna be cooped up in here all day. You can ride, but I don't wanna hear you bitching if you see some people get hurt."

Asha considered that and told him, "It's okay. I wanna go. I promise I won't say nothing."

They ate breakfast and left together at nine a.m. Boom headed to a neighborhood on the north side of town. Unexpectedly, he came to a stop on a quiet street and began to back into the driveway of a small home.

He told Asha, "Look in the glove compartment and click that garage door opener."

Asha did as she was told and was surprised to see the garage activate behind them.

"*This* is your house too?"

"You asking too many questions," Boom said as he backed up next to a Charger that was already in the garage. Other than this car being red and the other black, it was the same as the one he had at his *other* house.

"I'm just saying," Asha commented. "You have a lot of houses – or access to a lot of houses. Cars too. Killing people pay that good?"

He didn't say anything.

She tried a different approach. "How many jobs you do each year?"

"About two or three a month."

"At twenty G's a pop?"

"That's for a basic job."

"So you make a minimum of..."

"Stop counting my money," he said as he put the SUV in park and killed the engine. "Come on."

They transferred to the muscle car and left the neighborhood, headed south. Asha thought they were headed straight to her apartment, but when they got off the freeway, Boom turned into a seedy motel and told her, "Take your apartment key off your keychain." While she worked to get it free, he said, "I'm finna pick up somebody."

"Who?"

"Not sure," he said. "A crackhead. Gotta be a female."

Asha frowned. "What for?"

"I need to use her. When she come up to the car, just go along with whatever story I tell her. If you don't have to say nothing at all, that's prolly better."

Asha was even more confused. "You need to use her for what?"

"To get in your apartment."

Her eyes told him that was not an explanation.

He shook his head and said, "Don't worry about it. You said you wanted to ride, not ask a bunch of questions."

He drove past the motel's office and stopped in the middle of the parking lot. He kept the engine running. They didn't have to wait long before a black woman Asha would describe as a prostitute – *an ugly one* – spotted the Charger and began to head their way. When she saw a woman in the car with Boom, she stopped in her tracks and started to head back the way she'd come. He beeped his horn and waved her over. Her eyes were suspicious as she walked to his side of the car. Boom rolled his window down and waited for her to come closer.

She stopped a good ten feet away from his door and peered into the vehicle. Asha had never seen the woman before, but the hooker appeared to hate her on sight.

"You working?" she asked Boom.

He shook his head. "Naw, but I need to holler at you."

"What, y'all po-lice?"

"Naw. I need help with something, and I'ma pay you to do it." He reached into his pocket and flashed a wad of bills.

The woman stepped closer. "What you need help with?"

"My girl need to get something out her apartment," he said. "But she behind on the rent. The landlord will be on her ass, if she see her on the property. I need you to go in there and get her laptop. She left it on the kitchen counter, right next to the door."

The woman frowned. She looked from Boom to Asha and then back to him. "What, y'all trying to steal some shit?"

"We ain't stealing," Boom said. "It's her apartment, and it's her laptop. We got the key." He reached for it without looking Asha's way, and she handed it to him.

"Why *you* can't get it?" the woman asked.

"'Cause the landlord know me. She'll start some shit if she see me *or* my girl."

"So y'all wanna get me locked up for something I ain't got nothing to do with?"

"You gon' be in and out in thirty seconds," Boom said. "I'ma give you fifty dollars for that."

He could tell by the flash in her eyes that she was in, but she eyed his stack again and got greedy.

She told him, "A hundred."

"Shit ain't worth no hundred dollars."

"A laptop worth *five* hundred dollars," she spat. "Plus she prolly got some personal shit on it that make it worth more. You want me to get it for you, you gimme a hundred dollars."

"A'ight, ol' scheming ass bitch. I'm a give yo ass a hundred dollars."

"I want half first, before I even get in the car."

"You know what, ho," Boom said, his features set in a scowl. "I'ma give you half of that shit first, but when we get to them apartments, you bet not try to run off with my money. I'll chase you down and choke the shit out of you. Don't think yo skinny ass can outrun me. I'ma knock every one of them teeth out yo nasty ass mouth if you don't come back with the laptop!"

Asha tried her best to keep her expression neutral, but it was hard not to react to what she was hearing. She thought the woman would be a fool to get in the car with them after he talked to her like that, but it was clear the woman was on drugs. And in the words of the late, great Rick James, cocaine is a helluva drug.

"Gimme the money," she said.

Boom passed it through the window, and the prostitute climbed into the backseat.

When they got to the apartments, Asha thought the gig was up when Boom needed her to direct him to her building.

The woman in the backseat said, "I thought that was your girlfriend. Now you don't know where she stay."

"I haven't been over here in a while," Boom offered.

"Yeah, right. Ain't no telling what kind of shit y'all got going on. You prolly don't even know that bitch. But I'ma get that laptop. Let me out."

On the outside of the vehicle, she asked, "What's the apartment number again?"

"Two-twenty-one," Asha told her.

"Alright. Y'all wait right here."

"We ain't going nowhere," Boom assured her.

He and Asha were quiet as they watched her mount the stairs and use the key to gain entry into the apartment. A minute later, they were still waiting for her to come out. Another minute passed, and she had not returned.

Boom put the car in gear and drove away.

Asha looked over at him, once again confused. "We leaving?"

"Naw, but it don't take that long to see there ain't no laptop on the kitchen counter."

He drove around the corner and headed for the main office. He pulled to a stop in the fire lane next to the mailboxes and unbuckled his seatbelt.

"Get behind the wheel," he said as he exited the car. "Leave the engine running. I might need you to get us out of here in a hurry when I get back."

Asha got out and went to the other side of the car. Boom took off on foot, heading back towards her apartment, only he cut through the buildings this time. Exasperated, Asha watched the rearview mirror for the next five minutes, wondering what the hell was going on and whether he would ever take the time to explain himself. She didn't think it was unreasonable for her to expect him to do so.

When she finally saw him returning to the vehicle, he was moving a lot quicker than she'd ever seen him, but not full out running.

He hopped in the passenger seat and said, "Go. You ain't gotta speed, but you need to get outta here."

Asha put the car in gear and got moving. She shot glances at Boom, who looked contemplative but never stressed.

"*Please tell me what's going on*," she pleaded. "What happened to that lady? Did you see her?"

"No," he said with a shake of his head. "But I know she dead."

"*What?*" A cold numbness shot through her body like a gunshot. "*Are you serious?*"

"I'm not positive," he said, still bafflingly conversational. "But I'm pretty sure. I'd bet my house on it."

CHAPTER EIGHT
BEN & JERRY

"Can you tell me why you think she's dead?" Asha asked. She was still driving and hadn't calmed down much since they left her apartments.

Boom grunted. "You said you weren't gonna be tripping if somebody got hurt."

"I'm not tripping." She realized her tone didn't match her words and tried to suppress her anxiety. "I'm just asking a question. Is it okay if we talk about it? According to you, there's a dead lady in my apartment. You don't think I deserve to know anything about it?"

"Alright," Boom said. "We can talk about it. We gon' be on the road for a while anyway."

"Where we going now?"

"Back to that house on the north side. We can't roll around in this car no more. Gotta switch back to the 'burban. Do you remember how to get there?"

"I can get us to the neighborhood. I may not remember the exact street."

"That's cool. You okay to drive, or you wanna pull over?"

"No, I'm okay."

As they neared the freeway, Boom told her, "I think that lady dead because while I was waiting for her to come out your apartment, somebody else came out – somebody I recognize. I think it was Ben, or maybe Jerry." He shook his head. "I get them motherfuckers confused, but I know it was one of them."

Asha had a million questions, but she kept her mouth closed. Thankfully, Boom didn't leave her hanging this time.

"Ben and Jerry got they name when some goons saw them at Steak and Shake eating ice cream one night. They was all boo'd up, like they was on a date, so everybody started calling them Ben and Jerry, you know, like the ice cream. After a while, them niggas accepted the names."

Asha had to purse her lips to keep from responding to that.

"They gay," Boom clarified. "But don't think them niggas sweet, just 'cause they sweet."

Asha could hold her tongue no longer. "It's some gay niggas trying to kill you?"

"That's exactly what I'm talking about. Everybody got an opinion on gay people, and I'm telling you right now, you need to reprogram yo brain when it comes to these two. It's a lot of niggas in the ground 'cause they underestimated them. A lot more ended up in the hospital with major stitches and staples for coming at Ben and Jerry the wrong way about they sexuality. My homie Booger told me something that I think is a good philosophy when it comes to them: Just because they smoke dicks don't mean they won't smoke yo ass."

Asha took a deep breath and blew it out slowly. "Okay. I get what you saying. But you gotta admit, this some wild shit."

"Oh, it is," Boom agreed. "No doubt. Ben and Jerry started as dope boys, worked their way up to enforcers for a dealer named Sherm, and a few years ago they got into the murder game. They respected hitters now. They ain't on my level, but they get the job done."

"Okay... And you said one of them was waiting in my apartment?"

Boom nodded. "Yeah. He didn't see me, but I saw him clearly. He was in your crib waiting for you to get home. That's why I wanted to send a female in there, so he would think it was you, at least for a minute. My guess is after he found out that ho wasn't you, he interrogated her and then came looking for my car. That's why I pulled around the corner, next to them mailboxes. As far as that woman, I know he wouldn't leave a witness behind."

"So you knew she was gonna die when we sent her up there?" Asha felt sick to her stomach.

"No. I hoped no one was there. But I had my suspicions."

"I know you said someone might get hurt, but I..." She sighed. "I didn't think it would be an innocent person. I feel like we sent her to her death. And the way you were talking to her..."

Boom watched her for a moment before saying, "I talked to her the way I did because I was playing a role. If I talked to her like I'm talking to you now, she wouldn't have believed me. No offense, but she was a ho, and that's how ho's are used to niggas coming at them.

"Did I send her to her death? Yeah, probably. Am I gonna shed a tear about it? Not at all. I get why you feeling some type of way, but you know this is what I do. I don't make a habit of hurting innocents. What happened to that

99

lady was an unintended consequence. And I didn't personally kill her, so I can't carry that burden. You can't be rolling with me, if you gon' start crying every time something like this happens. Matter of fact, I'ma drop you off at my place, while I make some more moves."

"I'm not crying."

"You on the verge."

"I don't want you to drop me off, especially not now."

"You still don't feel safe at my house?"

"Boom, there's somebody trying to kill me."

"They don't really want you. They after me."

"But they'll kill me to get to you. It's the same thing."

He shook his head. Unexpectedly, he said, "Tell me about your murder."

That seemed to come from nowhere. "Huh?"

"You say you got locked up for murder. Who you kill?"

"Oh, it..." She switched gears and considered her sins, rather than his. "Someone tried to rape me. They didn't come close to actually doing it, but that's what they wanted to do. I would've got off, if I had let them go further, but I didn't."

Boom frowned. "And you got the nerve to complain about the way *I* tell a story..."

"I wasn't finished." She brought a hand to her face and rubbed her temple. "I was at a club with some of my friends, and this guy was following us around, trying to buy us drinks. He gave me bad vibes. I wasn't feeling him at all, but I'm the one he zeroed in on. He kept asking if I wanted to dance. I told him I didn't, but he wouldn't stop following me – not like right behind me, but every time I looked up, he wasn't too far away. Then I made the mistake of leaving my drink on a table..."

Boom gave her a look.

"I know that was stupid," Asha said. "It wasn't for that long, but it was long enough. That nigga got me."

"He slipped something in it?"

She nodded. "I noticed it tasted a little weird, but I had drunk half of it by then. An hour later, I felt like I was gon' pass out. My stomach was hurting too, so I thought the bar was serving cheap liquor. I told my friends I was sick, and I was gonna take off."

"They didn't walk you to your car?"

"The security at that club was on some ho-shit that night; talking 'bout no in-and-out. They said they'd charge my friends again if they tried to come back in, so I told them I was okay to leave on my own. I threw up before I made it to my car. My head cleared up a little, and when I got behind the wheel, I saw the dude that had been following me. That's when I knew what happened. I could've drove off..."

Asha's eyes were transfixed and unblinking on the road ahead of her.

"I didn't have to kill that man," she said. "But I was so pissed, thinking about what he wanted to do to me – what he prolly done before, to who knows how many girls. My anger started to build up, and I used it as fuel. The prosecutor said I lured him to my car. She was right. I could've left, or I could've locked my doors. But I waited for him. I waited for him to open my door. I acted like I was too out of it to resist when he tried to pull me out and put me in the backseat. And then I popped him. Twice in the chest."

She looked over at her passenger. "Like I said, the judge thought I had extenuating circumstances, so he only gave me ten years."

Boom nodded. "I'm surprised you got any time for that."

"I would've walked, if I had let him rip my clothes off first," Asha said. "The prosecutor said a man trying to pull me out of my car didn't give me an excuse to execute him. Just 'cause I *thought* he was trying to rape me doesn't mean he really was. She said he might have been trying to see if I needed help. Plus I didn't have proof that he was the one who put something in my drink."

"That's bullshit."

"I know. But there wasn't no witnesses. All they had was me with a gun and a dead guy in the parking lot. The prosecutor didn't buy my side of the story, so I got convicted."

Boom was quiet for a few seconds.

"The bottom line is," Asha continued, "I ain't scared to pull the trigger, if it comes to it. I don't want you to think I can't take care of myself or I won't have your back."

"You saying all this to say you want me to take you with me?"

She nodded. "I don't wanna be alone in your house, not knowing what's going on. Somebody trying to kill both of us, so we in this together."

He considered that before saying, "Alright, Asha. We'll see how it goes..."

Boom stopped at a few more locations before he finally got a lead. The first spot was the Butler Housing Projects on the outskirts of the bustling downtown area. Asha waited in the car, while he entered one of the brick buildings that were constructed to provide respite for the city's impoverished but had become a breeding ground for gangs, dealers and addicts.

When Boom returned to the SUV, he told her, "I think I might have something. Gotta go holler at Big Hooch."

"*Big Hooch?*"

"Don't ask me how he got that name."

Big Hooch wasn't at the place he usually retreated to after a long day of hustling, and he wasn't at his most popular dope spot on Jessamine. But one of the dealers there informed Boom of his whereabouts.

He returned to the car and told Asha, "Big Hooch in the hospital. I gotta go pay him a visit. And *no*, you can't go with me this time."

She didn't argue with him, but she asked, "What he got to do with this?"

"Hooch is a big timer," Boom explained. "He hired me for a job a little while ago. I think he might be running his mouth."

Asha knew what fate awaited the big timer, if that was the case. "What's wrong with him?" she asked. "You know why he in the hospital?"

"I don't know the specifics," Boom said. "But they say he was involved in some kind of fire. Big Hooch done got himself all burned up."

Asha cringed. She didn't know how to respond to that.

"When you get a chance," Boom said, "you need to call your people and tell them not to pop up at your apartment. I don't know if you already got a *Call before you come* policy. If not, this a good time to start one."

"Okay," Asha said. Her heart froze as she considered what could've happened if Gloria had showed up at her place, rather than the prostitute. "I'll let 'em know."

"What you gon' tell 'em?" Boom asked.

"I don't know, but I'll think of something."

When they returned to his home, Boom went to his bedroom and remained there for over an hour. Asha took that time to make her phone calls. Her sister was curious but didn't ask too many questions when Asha told her not to stop by without calling. Her cousin Tristan knew something was up.

"What's going on? Where you gon' be?"

"Just kicking it with some friends."

"You made some new friends, or is it somebody I know?"

"Why you asking so many questions?"

"You the one called me, telling me not to stop by. You in some kind of trouble?"

"Why you assuming something is wrong?"

"'Cause yesterday you said you was scared to meet that nigga Boom. Now you telling me don't go to your house. If it's something going on, you need to tell somebody, especially if it got something to do with that dude. That ain't the kind of problem you need to be dealing with on your own."

"There's no problem, Tristan. I'm just not gon' be around, that's all."

"You found you a new boyfriend or something?"

"No," Asha said, then decided that wasn't a bad idea. "I mean, he not my boyfriend. We just started talking."

"Oh. Why you didn't just say that? I'll give y'all some space. I don't wanna come knocking on the door, while you in there fucking." He laughed.

"Alright, man. Whatever."

When Boom emerged from his bedroom, Asha was not completely surprised to see a stranger walk by her bedroom door. She left the room to follow him. In the kitchen, she saw that his beard was gone again. He was now cleanshaven with a full head of hair. It was styled in cornrows. His dress was preppy, with a short-sleeve button down and khakis. He even wore a pair of glasses.

"I don't believe in nothing no more," Asha said as she walked around him, taking in his new persona. "We prolly never even had a black president. That was some white dude in blackface, wasn't it?"

Boom shook his head but didn't crack a smile. She could tell he was focused on whatever plans he had for Big Hooch.

He said, "Here," and placed a handgun on the counter. It was an all-black 9mm. "You know how to work that?"

"Turn the safety off, cock it and shoot," she said, matching his seriousness.

He looked her in the eyes. "Don't point that thing at me when I get back, like you did with that knife. I don't care how scared you are. Don't ever raise a gun to me."

"I won't."

She noticed he was carrying a small, leather pouch. She didn't ask what was in it.

He told her, "Alright, I'm out," and left without another word.

Forty minutes later, Boom arrived on the Trauma ICU unit at Jackson Memorial. He'd called the hospital's help desk from the parking lot and was told George Sanders, AKA Big Hooch, was in room 202. Boom walked past the nurses' station like he had every right to be there and didn't gather any suspicious stares from the hospital staff.

He entered Big Hooch's room and found his acquaintance lying in bed with his arms and chest heavily bandaged. There may have been more bandages on his lower extremities, but a blanket was pulled up to his stomach. His arms rested on elevation pillows. His head was bandaged, but not his entire face. Boom saw that what he'd heard was true. Hooch looked like he crawled out of a fireplace.

His eyes were closed, but they opened quickly when Boom approached the bed and said, "Wake up."

Big Hooch didn't seem surprised to see him there. His big chest rose and fell as he sighed, seemingly resigned to his fate.

"What the hell happened?" Boom asked.

After a few moments, Hooch said, "What it look like?"

Due to the damage his lips had taken, his speech was almost unintelligible, but Boom heard him just fine.

He asked, "Who did it?"

Hooch didn't say anything.

"Look like you on yo death bed," Boom said. "You gon' take yo street code all the way to the grave?"

Again, no response.

"I already know who did it," Boom bluffed. "What I wanna know is why you let them faggots do you like this."

What was left of Hooch's nostrils flared. The only part of his face that was still normal were his eyeballs. The sight of those perfect orbs floating in a wasteland of a head was enough to turn your stomach. But Boom had seen and inflicted damage that was just as bad, sometimes worse. He was unfazed.

"You know them punks ain't to be fucked with," Hooch said. "You ain't finna have me thinking I'm less of a man because it was them. They done took out way harder niggas than me and you."

"Who sicced 'em on you?" Boom wanted to know.

Hooch shook his head. "You know I don't know. And you know they won't never tell."

Boom believed that. A true hitter would take the death penalty before revealing who paid him to do a job.

"They come after you for that King David shit?"

Boom already knew the answer to that, but it was good to see Big Hooch confirm it by nodding.

"I told you that was a dumb hit," Boom said. "I told yo ass."

"Nigga, you the one who killed him."

"Don't put that shit on me. You wanted that man dead, and I told you it was a bad move. You was KD's biggest rival. I told you everybody in the hood would know it was you the second his body hit the floor. But no. Yo ass got greedy.

"For you to lay there and blame me lets me know you still on some dumb shit. That's like telling a contractor to build a bathroom in your front yard and then getting mad when you see how stupid it look. I did the job you paid me for, so it's on you. You need to own that."

If Big Hooch could move any of the muscles in his face, he would've fixed a hard glare on his hitman.

"And then you make this shit worse by putting my name it," Boom said.

Big Hooch shook his head. "I didn't give you up."

"Ain't no sense in lying. Ben and Jerry snatched you and lit yo ass up like a Christmas tree, and you gave me up. It's alright though. I bodied both of 'em."

Hooch's chest shuddered. "That, that's why I did it," he said. "I knew you could handle yourself, if they came for you. That's why I wasn't worried about telling them."

Boom was not surprised that his interrogation tactics had worked yet again. You'd be surprised how many truths you could get by telling lies.

"Why they didn't kill you?" he asked.

"They, they tried to. After burning me, they choked me. I passed out. I guess they thought I was dead, but I woke up when they was gone."

Boom nodded. First the hitman duo shot up his safe house without making sure they got him. Then they burned and choked Big Hooch but didn't make sure he was dead. Boom would never underestimate Ben and Jerry, but they'd made two crucial mistakes.

"Alright," he said. "I'm glad they didn't kill you, but that still leaves us with the *you* problem. You snitched on me Hooch. You know I can't let that fly."

"What? Nigga, I'm in this bed because of you. That's why I'm all burnt up, 'cause I wouldn't give 'em your name."

Boom shook his head. "No, you in this bed because you killed King David. Before you go meet your maker, you need to own that shit."

"But I took all that torturing 'cause I wouldn't give them yo name!"

"Don't raise your voice. I understand you got tortured, but you still fucked around and told them it was me. I can't let that slide."

Boom slowly unzipped the pouch he was carrying. He removed a needle and a vial that contained a clear liquid. "Don't worry," he said as he inserted the syringe and filled it all the way. "I ain't gon' make you suffer."

109

Big Hooch turned and stared at him as Boom approached his IV. Rather than reach for the bag dripping overhead, Boom went straight to the IV line in Hooch's arm.

Hooch's big chest rose and fell at a quickened pace. Finally he released a heavy sigh.

"Fuck it," he said. "I don't wanna live like this anyway. This ain't no life."

"Naw, it ain't," Boom agreed. "Yo kids would be scared to look at you."

Hooch didn't have eyebrows to pull off the cold look he was going for, but Boom got the message.

When he inserted the needle in the IV line, Hooch said, "You sure it ain't gon' hurt?"

Boom shook his head. "You ain't gon' feel a thing. You gon' fall asleep. Thirty minutes after that, it'll all be over."

He pushed the plunger slowly, until all of the poison had been dispensed. When he was done, Boom capped the needle and casually returned his supplies to the leather pouch. None of the nurses looked his way when he walked out of the room and headed for the elevator.

CHAPTER NINE
ACE IN THE HOLE

Boom knew he was being followed when he left the trauma unit, and he knew it wasn't the hospital security. When he exited the elevator on the ground floor, he walked casually as he counted the seconds before the stairway door opened and closed behind him.

Fifteen seconds.

He was twelve yards ahead of his pursuer by then. Twelve yards and fifteen seconds.

Boom did not look back as he exited the hospital and walked to the parking garage. He was parked on the 4th floor. He took the elevator, as any normal person would, but he knew the person on his tail would take the stairs. He also knew they planned to accost him in the garage, and they would sprint up the stairs to shorten the space between them.

When the elevator opened on the fourth floor, Boom stepped to the left and waited behind a pillar next to the stairway. He heard quick footsteps ascending the concrete steps. He reached to the small of his back and removed a Sig Sauer he had concealed under his shirt. The stairway door pushed open five seconds later. When the man pursuing him stepped out, Boom moved in behind him.

"Don't try nothing stupid," he said as he closed the distance and pushed the barrel of the pistol into his spine.

The man stopped in his tracks. He looked back but did not register the fear one would expect when you pull a gun on them. The man had long hair, styled in dreads, pulled back and secured with a rubber band. He wore an Adidas track suit with sneakers. He was tall and slim. His face was cleanshaven.

"Where yo pistol?" Boom asked him.

His hand moved. Boom shoved his gun deeper into his back.

He told him, "Don't reach for it, dumb ass."

The man told him, "It's in the front."

Boom reached around him and pulled it from his waistband. He flipped the safety on before stuffing it in his front pocket.

"Start walking," he told him.

The man did as he was told. He asked, "What you thinking, Boom? You know you fucking up, right?"

"*I'm* fucking up? You the one on the wrong end of the gun. And you let Big Hooch live... Y'all can't get shit right."

"We let him live on purpose. I knew you'd come for him."

"So you used Hooch as bait to draw me out?"

"Worked, didn't it?"

"This part of your plan too?" Boom asked. "Turn left up here."

"This ain't going exactly as we wanted," the man admitted. "But it'll do. Everything still working out for us."

Boom used his keys to chirp his Suburban's alarm. "Head that way."

"What, I'm supposed to get in that truck?"

"You don't have to. I can finish this right here."

"You not gon' do that," the man said assuredly. "You think you got the upper hand, but I got an ace in the hole."

"An ace in the hole, huh?"

"Yessir."

"Go over to that side," Boom said, directing him to the passenger side of his truck. "Open the back door."

The man followed his instructions.

"Reach under the seat," Boom told him. "Grab me one of them zip ties."

"You ain't finna put that shit on me."

"Why not? You got an ace in the hole, right? What you worried about?"

"You gon' lose," the man said. "I know you think you got everything figured out, but you ain't gon win this time."

"You prolly right," Boom said. "My luck gotta run out at some point. Grab me one of them zip ties."

The man bent and retrieved it.

"Put your hands behind your back," Boom ordered.

The man sighed heavily before complying. Boom had to tuck his gun behind his back to secure the zip tie, but he wasn't worried about the unarmed man trying anything. He had fifty pounds on him. He could snap the dread head's neck with minimal effort.

Once he was restrained, Boom told him, "Get in."

The man turned towards him before sitting in the car. They sized each other up once they were face to face.

"Which one are you?" Boom asked. "Ben or Jerry?"

"Ben." He studied Boom's features. "How you get them cornrows like that? That's a wig?"

"Something like that."

"That shit nice," Ben said. "Look real. You wear glasses, or those lens ain't real either?"

"Naw, they not real," Boom said. "Just glass."

"You do a good job with them outfits," Ben said. "You should get you a job working for a movie or something."

Boom chuckled. "Y'all after me for what happened to King David?"

"We just doing our job. You know how that is."

"Who hired you?"

"You know that conversation dead."

"Big Hooch the one killed KD. You could've finished your job when you burned him up."

"Our job is to get him and whoever pulled the trigger. We knew he didn't do it himself. Thanks for taking care of him, by the way. I was gonna come back for him after I took care of you. You did half our job for us."

"But now you tied up, and you ain't got no way to take me out," Boom said. "So how you figure I ain't winning?"

Ben grinned. "I told you Boom. I got an ace in the hole. Why don't you call Jerry for me? Put him on speaker. You'll see what I'm talking about."

Boom grinned too. "Okay, nigga. I'll bite. Move your legs, so I can close this door."

Ben scooted back in the seat and turned, until his long legs were facing forward. Boom closed the door and walked around to the driver's side. He placed Ben's gun on the passenger seat and removed his cellphone from his pocket before starting the car.

"Okay," he said without looking back. "What's Jerry's number?"

Ben gave it to him. "Put him on speaker."

"I heard you." Boom dialed the number. The sound of the phone ringing blared through the truck's speakers. Someone answered after a couple of rings.

"Who dis?"

"Yo, it's me," Ben called from the backseat.

After a pause, Jerry said, "What number is this you calling from?"

"We got a little issue," Ben said. "I'm in Boom's car. He got me tied up. We talking on speaker. He listening."

Another pause, then, "*Let 'em go,*" Jerry growled.

"Now why would I do that?" Boom said. "Y'all trying to kill me. The way I see it, the best thing for me to do right now is pop your boyfriend and then come find you. You wanna listen to me kill him?"

"*You bet not touch him.*" Jerry's voice was low and guttural. "How you let him snatch you?" he asked Ben.

"We'll talk about that later," his boyfriend said.

"Let me guess," Boom interrupted. "If I let him go, you'll pinkie promise not to kill me..." He enjoyed pushing Jerry's buttons.

The man on the phone said, "Shit ain't funny."

From the backseat, Ben said, "Hey, baby, tell him where you at. He don't think I got an ace in the hole."

"I don't give a fuck about yo ace," Boom said.

"*You* may not," Jerry said through the speaker, "but what about yo bitch? You think she care about somebody name Gloria Turner on Meadowcrest Drive?" He gave him an address.

In the backseat, Ben started snickering.

"Gloria is Asha's sister," Jerry clarified. "Let Ben go *right now*, or I'ma run up in this house and kill everythang moving. It's a blue Camry and a black Tahoe in the driveway, so I know the whole family home. Think real hard about yo next move, 'cause if you hurt baby, I'ma black out. Shit gon' get *real* bloody."

Boom feigned nonchalance with a bored sigh. "Lemme call Asha, see if she even care about them people. I know I don't." He hung up on him.

In the backseat, Ben was chuckling. "Told you, nigga."

"Y'all ain't talking about shit," Boom said. Rather than call Asha with the same phone, he grabbed another one from the center console. He dialed her number, and she answered right away. The Bluetooth wasn't activated on this cell, so she wasn't on speaker.

"Hello? Boom?"

"Yeah, it's me."

"Is everything okay?"

"I don't know," he said. "Do you know somebody named Gloria who lives on Meadowcrest?"

She inhaled sharply. "Yeah. That, that's my sister. Wha, why you ask me that?"

"What kind of cars are in her driveway?"

"Wha, what? *Boom, what's going on?*"

"Calm down and answer the question."

"They got a Camry and a, and a uh, a Tahoe. Wha–"

"Listen to me," he said. "I got Ben in the backseat of my car. He tied up. His boyfriend is outside your sister's house. He say he gon' run up in there and kill everybody if I don't let this nigga go."

"*Then let him go!*"

116

"Listen to me," Boom said. "I need you to go to the kitchen and look in the drawer next to the dishwasher. It's a gun in there. I think these niggas might come for you, if this shit go bad."

Asha couldn't have been more confused. Her voice rattled when she said, "Boom, you already gave me a gun."

"Stop panicking and *listen to me*. Go to the kitchen and look in that drawer. Do it now."

Asha's legs almost gave out when she hopped out of bed, but she managed to make it to the kitchen. There was no gun in the drawer, only two sets of car keys.

"You got the gun?" Boom asked.

"*Boom, it's just keys in here...*"

"Keep that gun on you," he said. "I'm finna call this other nigga. I'll get back to you after I figure out what we gon' do."

"*Boom, please...*"

"A'ight. Keep your phone close to you... *Wait – don't hang up!*" He smacked his lips in frustration. "Dumb bitch hung up," he said to the man in the backseat.

He checked the display on the phone as he placed it in his lap. The call was still active. Boom grinned inwardly, wondering whose ace in the hole would prevail. Jerry was a stone-cold killer, but Asha was driven by the need to protect her family. Those were powerful emotions. He hoped it would give them the edge.

He called Jerry back on the other phone, once again on speaker.

He answered with, "You called her?"

"Yeah," Boom said. "Like I said, I don't give a fuck about the people in that house, but my girl does. So I guess

117

neither one of us has the upper hand. So, what's the play?" He looked down at his other phone. The call was still active.

"Let baby go, and I'll drive off," Jerry said. "We'll go our separate ways."

"Yeah right. You'll still be trying to kill me or hurt Asha's family. That don't seem like a win to me."

"You ain't gon' win, Boom. Not this time," Jerry said.

"I told him," Ben called from the backseat.

"Why don't you give me Asha's purse," Boom said. "You got access to too much of her personal information. I'll trade you Ben for that purse, and we'll all walk away – for now. I know you still gon' be trying to get me, and I'll be looking for y'all too. But as far as today, we'll call it even."

"You gon' trade Ben for this purse?"

"Yep. And you gotta give me your word that you'll leave Asha out of this."

"Bet. Meet me at–"

"Naw, you been calling too many shots," Boom said. "I decide where we meet."

He checked to make sure Asha was still on the other call before he directed him to an underpass. Jerry wasn't familiar with the location, but he said he could find it.

"Meet me there at noon," Boom said.

"A'ight." Then he asked Ben, "Baby, you alright?"

Boom disconnected before his hostage could respond and then he turned and looked at him. "How y'all find Asha's sister anyway?"

"We looked that bitch up on Facebook," he revealed. "Yo girl's profile ain't even private. She got damn near her whole family tree on there. That bitch dumb as a box of rocks."

"Yeah, she ain't too bright," Boom said.

He looked down at his other phone. Asha was still on the line. He waited a couple of seconds, and she disconnected.

Boom didn't speak much to his captive on the way to the underpass. Ben was careful not to say anything that would piss him off, and Boom was annoyed by his lack of fear. The man had been captured and restrained in the backseat of his enemy's car. Would it kill him to show a little humility?

When he turned under the interstate, he saw a white Highlander waiting for them. He pulled to a stop behind it and asked Ben, "That's baby?"

"Yeah, that's him," he said as he peered through the front window. "Leave yo gun in the car."

"He ain't gon' leave his gun in the car."

"Call him. I'll tell him to."

Boom shook his head, but he made the call. Jerry answered right way.

"What's up."

"Baby," Ben said. "This us behind you. Boom finna get out, and he gon' leave his gun. You leave yours too."

"A'ight," Jerry said.

"Bring the purse," Boom told him before disconnecting.

He waited for Jerry to exit his truck before he did the same. His adversary was tall and slim like his boyfriend. His hair was also styled in dreads, but they weren't as long. Jerry had Asha's purse in one hand and nothing in the other. Boom thought about killing him then, but Jerry didn't step away from his open car door. A shootout might ensue if he saw Boom reaching, so he didn't try anything.

The men walked towards each other. The traffic from the freeway overhead echoed in the underpass. The stench from illegally dumped trash bags and other debris was almost overwhelming. Boom didn't doubt that someone had discarded a dead dog down there.

When the men were within six feet, they both came to a stop. Jerry looked past the hulking killer to make sure his mate was in the car and safe before a smile curved his lips.

He said, "Boom, you losing your touch."

Boom's features remained rigid. "How you figure?"

"You trading a whole nigga for a purse. What kind of sense that make?"

"Just trying to keep my woman and her family safe."

"How is getting this purse back gonna accomplish that? You don't think I remember where Gloria stay?"

"You said you'd give me your word."

"Boom, you know we trying to kill you right? Why the hell would you believe anything I say to you?" He shook his head, surprised that this wasn't obvious.

"So, what you saying is I can't trust you. Your word don't mean nothing."

"You wanna know how much you can trust me?" Jerry dropped the purse and reached in his waistband.

Boom remained still as he drew his weapon. If not for another car turning into the underpass, Boom had no doubt the man would've ended his life. But Jerry was momentarily distracted. He transferred his gun to his left hand and held it at his side, hoping the bystander would pass through and see nothing amiss. Just two men having a friendly conversation under a bridge. Nothing to see here.

But the black Charger didn't continue on its merry way. It came to a stop next to them. The window tint prevented them from seeing who was inside, but the driver didn't waste any time rolling it down. Asha already had her gun raised, pointed squarely at Jerry. She had come to a stop less than ten feet away from them. Boom didn't know if she was a good shot, but he didn't think she could miss at that distance. He smiled, looking back at Jerry.

"Did you really think I'd let you kill me?"

Jerry looked from Asha to Boom.

"I know what you thinking," Boom said. "You can get her first and then me. The problem with that is she's on your right, and your gun's on your left. You can't swing your arm over there before she let off at least two. You might be able to get me, but she gon' still get you, and then she gon' kill Ben."

The hitman's dark skin turned gray right before Boom's eyes.

"Alright. Then we'll do it like we said," he bargained. "You gimme Ben for the purse."

Boom shook his head, still grinning. "You think I'm finna trade a whole nigga for a purse?" Without looking her way, he said "Asha, this the man that was parked in front of your sister's house. He didn't have no problem killing the whole family thirty minutes ago."

"I wasn't gon' do it," Jerry said. "It was just a threat."

"Asha," Boom said. "He 'bout to make a move. If I was in your shoes, and this man knew where my sister lived, I'd kill him right now."

A fresh coat of sweat glossed Jerry's forehead. His eyes darted as he sought a way out. "We can squash this whole thing right now. I – I don't want no more beef. Fuck the money. I don't care about this job. Just, just let Ben go, and we done. I swear we ain't gon' come after y'all."

"*Asha*," Boom said. "This nigga 'bout to make a move."

"*No, I ain't,*" Jerry squealed. "*I ain't gon do nothing.*" He looked into the Charger and appealed to her directly. "I ain't gon' do nothing. This done."

"Drop yo gun then," Boom said.

The wild eyes snapped back to him. Beads of sweat began to trickle down Jerry's forehead.

Boom began to doubt his ace for the first time. "*Asha–*"

PAP! PAP! PAP!PAP! PAP!

Jerry's body twisted at grotesque angles as the hot rocks flung him to the ground.

"*NOOOOOOOOOO!*"

The scream came from the backseat of Boom's SUV. Ben leaned forward, almost all the way to the front seat, staring at the carnage. The look on his face was the epitome of devastation.

Boom bent to retrieve Jerry's gun and the purse before he looked back at the Charger. Asha wore a look of stunned disbelief.

She snapped out of it when he told her, "Good job. Now you need to get gone. I'll meet you back at the house."

She didn't take off immediately. She was still watching when Boom walked over to Jerry's body and put two more in his head, just in case.

BLAK! BLAK!

"*STOOOOOP! NOOOOOOOOOO!*"

Asha took off then.

Boom returned to the Suburban and tried to tune out the screams belting from the backseat as he fled the scene.

CHAPTER TEN
FIRST TIME

Boom was okay with Ben screaming and crying in the backseat, but he drew the line when he lie on his back and started kicking the door, the window and finally Boom's headrest.

"I'ma kill you, Boom! You killed baby! I swear before God I'ma kill you!"

Boom dodged the size twelve Adidas as best he could as he exited the freeway. He knew a few good killing spots in just about every neighborhood in the city, but most of them weren't in play in broad daylight. He settled on a quiet street with more vacant houses than occupied ones.

He pulled into a park that was overgrown and desolate at that hour, due to the intense afternoon heat. Ben's feet were facing the driver's side, so Boom walked around the vehicle. Ben tried to swivel his body in time to deliver a few kicks to the choppers when Boom opened the door, but he didn't make it in time.

Boom snatched the back door open and quickly caught him in a rear chokehold. Ben continued to kick like a mad man, but his legs could do no harm from this position. Plus his arms were firmly secured behind his back.

"If you tell me who hired you, I'll you let live," Boom told him.

"*Nigga, you lying!*"

"I give you my word."

"*Fuck you, Boom! I'll see yo ass in hell!*"

Even as he applied enough pressure to put the man to sleep, Boom admired him for not snitching. He continued to squeeze his adversary's neck after Ben passed out. He held the chokehold until he knew the man was good and dead.

When he returned home, he found Asha waiting for him in the kitchen. She sat at the table perusing her cellphone, but not really paying attention to anything she saw. She watched Boom as he went to the sink to wash his hands. He then took a seat across from her. He rested his large forearms on the table, and they stared at each other for a few moments.

Finally he asked, "You alright?"

She nodded. Her expression was deadpan. Her eyes lacked focus.

"Do you regret what happened?" he asked.

She met his eyes. She shook her head but said, "I don't know."

"I pushed you to do that," he said. "I know it wasn't right to put you in that position. But when I found out Jerry was at your sister's house, I didn't have a choice. If I would've killed Ben, Jerry would've ran up in that house. If I had let Ben go, they'd both still be after us, and they'd know where your sister stays. You already know they don't have a problem taking out an innocent to get what they want."

Asha nodded. "But do you think he was telling the truth when he said he didn't care about the hit no more."

"A man will say anything to save his life," Boom replied. "Would I put my life on the line for a scared man's promise? Nope. Only a fool would, as far as I'm concerned."

Asha sighed. "Okay. Then we did what had to be done."

Boom continued to watch her.

She asked him, "What about the other one, the one you had tied up?"

"He still in the truck."

Asha's eyes widened. "*In the garage*?" Her attention moved in that direction.

"He dead," Boom said. "I had to choke him on the way over here."

Asha's mouth fell open. She blinked a few times before closing her mouth without speaking.

"I was gonna kill him anyway," Boom offered. "Wasn't sure how, but there was no way that man could continue to walk the earth after what we did to his boyfriend. He would've burned the whole city down to find us."

Asha nodded. She knew he was telling her right, but that didn't stop the world from sinking beneath her. She felt like evil spirits were flowing through her veins, rather than blood.

"What happened at the hospital?" she asked. "You went to see Big Hooch, and the next thing I know we're headed to the underpass."

"Let me break this whole thing down for you..."

Asha's eyes had returned to the garage door. He waited until she was looking at him again.

"You worried about that body?" he asked.

"I... It's just..."

"I get it," he said. "It's a little unnerving to know it's a dead man out there."

She nodded. "Yeah. It is."

"I gotta dump him, but I can't do it till nightfall. You gon' be okay with knowing he out there till then?"

She shrugged. "I guess I don't have a choice."

"I know I'm taking you too fast. I'm sorry."

"No, it's alright. Tell me about Big Hooch."

"Yeah, so this all started when Hooch hired me to kill a man named King David. He go by KD. KD and Hooch were both big timers. They tried not to compete for the same customers or real estate, but they both wanted to expand, and a war popped off. I told Hooch everybody on KD's team would know it was him, if I took that job. But he wasn't taking no for an answer. He would've paid somebody else to do it if I didn't, so I took out KD."

Asha swallowed and nodded

"As I expected," Boom said, "somebody on KD's side finally decided to go after Hooch for that killing. They hired Ben and Jerry, and they got hold of Hooch and tortured him, burned him up pretty bad. But they didn't only want Hooch for the killing. Whoever hired them also wanted the man who pulled the trigger. Hooch fucked around and told them it was me."

Asha was listening intently. She didn't have any questions.

"I went and saw Hooch to confirm what I already knew," Boom said. "After he admitted to giving up my name, I had to take him out."

"You killed him in the hospital?"

Boom nodded. "The hospital's as good a place as any."

Asha suspected the means of death had something to do with the leather pouch Boom had that morning, but she didn't ask.

"Ben was waiting for me at the hospital," Boom said. "He knew I'd come for Hooch. But I got the drop on him, and that's where you came in. You know the rest from there."

"So, um..." Asha sighed. "This ain't the end of it, is it?"

Boom shook his head. "No. I gotta find out if Ben and Jerry told anyone what Hooch said about me being the triggerman. And I gotta find out who hired them."

"What are you gonna do when you find out?"

"I gotta take 'em out," Boom said matter-of-factly. "It's been my experience that if you hire a hitter to do a job, and he don't accomplish the mission, you hire another hitter."

Asha understood that. "How will you find out?"

"I got my ways. I'ma take off later, when it's dark."

"You mean *we*..."

He frowned at her. "I don't need you to come with me."

"Why you always trying to kick me to the curb? I killed a man today. If that don't put me in it just as much as you, I don't know what does."

"Just because you in it don't mean I need you to help me finish it."

"I didn't say you needed me, but I don't wanna be by myself tonight, after everything that's happened."

"I work better alone."

"You didn't work better alone when that man pulled a gun on you in the underpass." She stood angrily. "Are you hungry?"

Boom watched her with a confused expression. "Yeah. I can eat."

She went to the fridge to see if there was something she could put together.

While eating a frozen pizza – Boom truly needed to make a trip to the grocery store – Asha came to terms with their circumstances and accepted the steps they needed to take to bring this to a conclusion.

Boom asked her, "Do you think you could kill again, if it came down to it."

She nodded. "Yeah, I think so."

"That kind of answer is the main reason I don't wanna take you with me tonight. If my life is on the line, I don't wanna have no doubt that you got my back."

"I had your back today."

"Yeah, after I practically *begged* you to kill that man. It's hard to train somebody in this shit. That's why I don't like working with people."

"You *begged* me to kill him?"

"Yeah. I said, '*Asha, this is the man that was parked in front of your sister's house. He didn't have no problem killing the whole family thirty minutes ago.*'"

"That was you telling me to shoot?"

"Yeah. And yo ass sitting there looking crazy, not picking up on what I'm saying. Then I said, '*Asha, he 'bout to make a move. If I was in your shoes, and this man knew where my sister lived, I'd kill him right now.*'"

She took a deep breath. "Okay. I thought you wanted me to kill him then."

"But you didn't do it."

"I wasn't sure."

"I told you he was about to make a move – *again* – and you didn't shoot."

Asha felt like a fool for wavering at that crucial moment. "Why didn't you just say shoot?"

"Because he would've made a move for sure. He probably would've shot me, before you had time to react."

"Well, couldn't you come up with some kind of code word, so I'll know next time?"

He laughed at that. She didn't think she'd ever seen him laugh. She liked the twinkle in his eyes, the curve of his full lips.

"What I'm supposed to say?" he asked. "Nigga, put that gun down. *Pineapple!*"

Asha laughed too. "It ain't gotta be nothing stupid like that."

He shook his head, chuckling.

"What about *your* first time?" she asked. "You pulled the trigger with no hesitation?"

His smile slipped and then went away completely. "Naw. My first time was a hot mess, way worse than what happened today."

Asha waited, wondering if he wanted to tell the story. He did.

"I was twenty-three," he recalled, "an all-around knucklehead with no direction in life. I'd just got out the Army—"

"You were in the military?"

He nodded. "Got an honorable discharge, but I didn't wanna reenlist. I went back to the hood and fucked around and started slanging for a dude named Monk. I wasn't feeling it, though. The dope game pays good, but that shit's for suckers, as far as I'm concerned. You either on a corner waiting for the laws to roll up, or you're in a dope house, waiting for the laws to kick the door in. If you ain't in either of those places, you rolling around with dope on you, waiting for a law to pull you over.

"I got arrested twice and was about to give that shit up for good when I got robbed by a dude named Spoon. I was gonna go after him, just to save face, but Monk put $5,000 on the nigga's head. My original plan was to whoop Spoon, but I figured I might as well kill 'em and take that five G's."

Asha nodded. She leaned towards him with her elbows on the table.

"It was raining the night I went after him," Boom continued. "It was cold too, so I was wearing a long trench coat. I picked that coat, 'cause I had a shotgun, and I could hold it under the coat without nobody seeing. I drove to the projects and waited for about an hour.

"When I saw Spoon's car pull up, I got out and started walking up to him. He saw me as soon as he got out his car.

He took off, and I took off after him. I was running through the projects with my shotgun in full view. He hit one of them corners, and I slipped and busted my ass trying to keep up. The shotgun fell out my hands and started sliding on that sidewalk..."

Boom's eyes stared past her as the memory filled his mind. "Spoon looked back, and he saw me on the ground, and he saw my gun. And I could see his mind working, wondering if he should go for the gun or keep running. He decided to go for it. We went for it at the same time. I got there first. I was still on the ground when I picked it up and let off the first shot. *Boom!*

"I hit 'em mid-center, but he didn't go down. He started fighting me for the shotty. With his hands all over it, I couldn't get it to cock again, so I started punching him. I didn't have my hands on the gun at that point. He could've shot me with it, but I got in a couple of good licks, and he fell back. The shotgun hit the ground again, and I snatched it up. I cocked it and put another one in his chest. *Boom!* I put one in his head. *Boom!* And then I took off."

Asha's eyes were wide and unblinking. Her heart stuttered each time he said, *Boom!*

"I didn't realize I was a bloody mess," Boom said, "till I got back to the dope house. They asked if I stabbed that nigga and wrestled with him while I was stabbing him. I learned some lessons that night."

"Like what?"

"First off, don't get too close to your target, if you don't have to. Second, don't put yourself in a position where you have to chase them. If they see you coming before you ready to pull the trigger, you fucking up. And most importantly, don't never let three or four niggas know you just killed somebody. I walked in that dope house proud of what I had done, not thinking that everybody in there was now a witness. I shouldn't have got away with that hit, but somehow I did. I don't move like that no more."

He rose to his feet. "So, compared to *my* first time, yours was damn near perfect. Your only problem was not shooting him sooner, but I understand why you hesitated. I'm 'bout to bathe and take me a nap. It's gonna be a long night."

"Okay," Asha said with a nod. She watched him walk out of the kitchen, and then her eyes returned to the garage door. She sighed as she left her seat and headed for the bedroom.

After removing his cornrows wig cap and undressing, Boom took a long, hot shower. But he never felt completely clean when he ended someone's life, especially after an up close and personal murder like Ben's. He climbed into bed but was unable to drift off to sleep. He was still awake twenty minutes later when he heard a light knocking on his door.

"What's up?" he called.

"You awake?" Asha asked.

"Yeah, I'm up."

"Can I come in?"

Boom's body was concealed by his sheets, but he warned her, "Yeah, but I'm in my boxers."

She opened the door, and he saw that she was in her sleepwear as well. He assumed she had underwear on underneath one of the tee shirts he bought her, but he couldn't be sure. The shirt wasn't very long. From the front, he caught the slightest glimpse of what *might* have been her panties. He forced himself not to stare as a pulse of energy descended from his chest, down into his boxers.

She was soft-spoken when she asked, "Can I get in bed with you?"

Boom was curious but not opposed to the move at all. This was the second time he got a look at her smooth, creamy legs. But other than when he tackled her to the floor at his safe house, he had never touched her.

He told her, "Yeah. If you want to."

She went to the opposite side of the bed and crawled in next to him. She got under the covers, and they lie side by side on their backs, still not touching. Boom looked her way, and then his gaze returned to the ceiling. She did the same.

"I know we supposed to be napping," she said. "But I can't sleep."

"You not gon' be able to," he said, "not after what happened."

Her head rolled towards him. "But you can?"

"Maybe. I think so."

When she didn't say anything, he said, "You wondering how..."

She nodded. "Yeah."

He took a deep breath. He had the covers pulled midway up his torso. His massive chest was in full view. Asha watched it rise and fall slowly.

"This murder game changes you," he said. "The first one is hard. You become engaged in spiritual warfare with your conscious, your god and everything you've been told throughout your life about right and wrong. The second one is easier. The one after that, even easier. By the time you get to where I am, you not at war with yourself anymore. You become at peace with who you are – *what* you are."

Asha was surprised by his insight.

"You need to think about that," he said, "before you try to roll out with me tonight. I don't think you know what you're getting yourself into."

"I do."

"You think you can go out and kill a few more people and then go back to putting up awnings again, like it ain't nothing?"

A few more people?

"I don't go back to work on Monday," she said. "I'm off all next week."

He said, "You can avoid my question, but you can't avoid your fate, if you come with me tonight."

"What's my fate, if I go?"

His head rolled towards her. He looked her dead in the eyes. "You'll never be the same."

His words sent a clap of thunder down her spine. She took a deep breath and then rolled to her side, facing him. She reached slowly, almost tentatively, and placed a hand on his chest.

"You got a woman?" she asked.

He continued to look into her eyes. "No."

Asha wasn't sure if she believed him or if it even mattered at that moment. Her eyes remained glued to his as her hand slid down his chest, over his abs and into his boxers. When he didn't stop her, she caressed his dick, which was already hardening. She stroked it softly before

135

pulling the sheets back as she scooted down on the mattress. His eyes followed her when she took him into her warm mouth. He inhaled sharply. She felt his legs stiffen as she pleasured him.

The sight of her head bobbing up and down in his lap had Boom rock hard in a matter of seconds. Her eyes slipped closed. She stroked his shaft and sucked him long and deep. When he first met her, Boom never dreamed he'd one day have her sweet lips wrapped around his dick. Now, he felt like there was nothing he wanted more.

Her eyes opened when she tasted his pre-cum. She saw that Boom was propped up on his elbows, watching her. He reached and gently halted her movements with a hand on her cheek. She thought his fingers would move to the back of her head and urge her to suck deeper and harder. But he pulled away. She respected his decision not to cum in her mouth, even though she was hoping he would do so.

She went in again, kissing and sucking the tip before asking, "You got a condom?"

Her breath on his bulging tip made his dick jump.

He nodded. His voice was husky. "In that dresser behind you. Top right drawer."

Asha slipped off the bed. She opened the drawer and found the contraceptive. With her back to him, she pulled her tee shirt over her head. Boom saw that she did have on a bra and panties. The sight of her ass in the panties he bought her made his dick throb even harder. She unfastened her bra and then slid the panties down her legs before turning to face him. Boom was amazed by how fine she was. This wasn't the dingy construction worker he'd first encountered. Asha was beautiful. From head to toe, her body was flawless.

She crawled on top of him and slid the condom down his shaft. She straddled him and used one hand to guide him into her oasis. Her chest hitched as she took him in. Her mouth parted as he penetrated her fully. She leaned forward and placed both hands on the bed, on either side of his head. Boom reached down and grabbed an ass cheek in each hand. He watched her eyes, her dark nipples, the tightening in her stomach as she began to ride him.

He hoped he'd outlast her, because he had a desire to roll her over and dominate the pussy. He knew it wouldn't be easy. Asha's stroke game was magical. The way she grinded on his dick made his head spin. Thankfully he felt her walls grip him tighter and begin to contract after a few minutes. The speed of her hips increased, and she moaned slightly as the trembling in her legs became spasms, and her body produced its essence as an offering.

Try as he might, the sight and feel of her cumming on his dick unraveled the last of his resolve. He gripped her ass and guided her hips to fuck him harder. His heartbeats were thunderous.

Through the rush of blood between his ears, he heard her whisper, "*You cumming?*"

Boom's lips parted. His breaths came in shudders. He nodded.

"*I feel you,*" she purred, still grinding, slower now. "*I feel you cumming. I feel it, Boom...*"

CHAPTER ELEVEN
SO MANY BODIES

Asha didn't sleep well. She didn't think she'd slept at all, but when her eyes fluttered open, Boom was out of bed, and the remnants of a nightmare lingered in her psyche, causing her to sit up with a start. She tried to remember what the dream was about but couldn't.

She heard Boom in the bathroom. She looked in that direction and saw him leaning over the counter. From her vantage point, she couldn't see what he was doing, but she knew he was looking in the mirror, doing something to his face.

As wonderful as their lovemaking was, the sight of him weighed heavily on her soul. She realized her life was spiraling out of control. She was falling for a killer, and because of him, she had murdered a man in broad daylight. She knew things could only go downhill from here, if she left with him tonight. But as a moth is drawn to a campfire that singes its wings, she felt compelled to follow this man, possibly through the gates of hell.

She climbed out of bed and found her bra and panties in front of the dresser. She put them on and approached the bathroom. Standing in the doorway, she saw that Boom was affixing his notorious beard. She saw that it was all one piece, with what had to be a strong adhesive on the inside. He watched her in the reflection as he made sure it was straight and looked natural.

"You change your mind about going with me?" he asked.

She shook her head.

"Go change then," he said. "Brush your hair back, as tight as you can. You gotta wear a wig."

That should have been startling, but it wasn't. Asha wondered if, because of him, everything was losing its shock value.

"Okay," she said and backed out of the restroom.

The wig he had for her was long and curly. Asha knew it was a woman's wig but couldn't bring herself to ask why he had it or who had worn it before her. Standing in his bathroom, he used an elastic strap to secure it. He then gave her three gold chains that were encrusted with diamonds. The necklaces looked too gaudy to be real, but she couldn't say for sure.

He finished her disguise by sticking a dark, protruding mole on her nose, above the left nostril. Asha cringed when she looked at herself in the mirror. The wig was okay, but the mole made her look like a witch.

"Boom, this is ugly. Why do I have to wear this?" she asked, fingering the rubber atrocity.

He told her, "You're not going to a beauty pageant."

"I know, but why do I have to wear something that makes me look ugly?"

"Because when people make a memory," he explained, "especially when they're under stress, they remember what stands out the most. You're not Asha right now. You're a bitch with long hair, a bunch of chains and a big-ass mole on your nose. That's the way I'd describe you, if I had to tell somebody what you look like."

Asha understood. "How do you know so much about disguises?"

"I don't really. But I know a lot about human nature. Knowing how people think is why I'm good at what I do. I don't wanna bring you into this, but if I do, the least I can do is protect your identity."

"Okay. Thank you."

Boom dressed in all black. He topped his outfit with a ball cap. In the closet, he had a plethora of weapons mounted on the wall. He selected a shotgun and pistol for himself. He grabbed another 9mm for Asha. This one was chrome.

"You don't want me to use the gun you gave me yesterday?" she asked.

He shook his head. "Naw. That gun got a body on it. We gotta burn it."

She nodded and took the new gun.

They headed for the garage, where Asha encountered her first body for the night. When Boom opened the door, the first thing that hit her was the stench. She never expected a corpse to smell pleasant, but she didn't think it would be so overpowering, after only ten hours.

"It was a hundred degrees today," Boom said, reading her expression. "This nigga pretty ripe."

"We gotta ride in the car with him?" Asha asked, frowning.

"No, you'll be spared this time. I need you to follow me in the Charger."

This time?

He tossed her the keys to the sports car.

They left the house at ten-thirty. Asha followed Boom to an east side neighborhood. He called her as they headed north on Riverside Drive.

He told her, "Go to that 7-11 up there and get some gas. There's two gas cans in the trunk of your car. Fill them up too."

Asha stopped at the gas station, and he continued on ahead of her. She knew he didn't come with her because he planned to burn the SUV with Ben's body in it. It wouldn't be good for him to be seen on the gas station cameras.

A few minutes later, she called him back after she was done pumping the gas.

He answered and said, "I'm up the street waiting on you. Keep heading the way we were going."

She caught up with him a few blocks down the road. She passed him and then slowed down, so he could get in front of her again.

He led her to Sycamore Park, which was nothing like she remembered it. She hadn't been there in over a decade. She knew the park had gone downhill since then, but nothing she'd heard prepared her for the degradation she observed when Boom turned off the main thoroughfare and drove down one of the park's winding roads.

It was clear the city had given up on the area and turned it over to Mother Nature and the neighborhood's undesirables. Few of the street lamps had working bulbs in them. The road they were traveling on was littered with broken glass and other debris. The overgrown vegetation was suffocating. Gang graffiti marred the damaged benches and gazebos.

Boom drove deep into the park and left the road unexpectedly. Asha followed him, wondering if he was choosing a spot indiscriminately. When he came to a stop in a clearing, she knew that he hadn't. She didn't think there was anywhere in the park where he could start a fire without burning a few acres in the process. But Boom had found a paved area that was roughly the size of a basketball court. Did he already scout this place? Asha was not surprised by his forethought, but she was constantly impressed with his planning.

She came to a stop twenty yards behind him and left the Charger running. In the glow of her headlights, Boom fully doused the SUV. He poured the majority of the gasoline on the body and the gun in the backseat. He used so much gas, Asha worried he'd lose his eyebrows and beard when he ignited it, but she realized this wasn't his first rodeo. Boom poured the last of the gas on the ground, creating a 10-foot-long trail that led away from the Suburban. Asha had never seen anyone do that in real life.

Before he bent to light it, he told her, "You can get in the car, on the passenger side."

She hesitated. "Is it okay if I watch?"

He frowned but didn't say anything. He lit his makeshift fuse line. In the darkness, the fire quickly skated across the concrete before encountering the SUV with a loud *WHOOMP*! The initial fireball seemed to light up the whole park. It licked the sky a full twenty feet above them. Asha was mesmerized. Boom casually returned to the Charger, as if this was something he did every Saturday night. He got in behind the wheel, and she slipped in beside him.

"I never seen anything like that," she breathed.

He nodded as he got them back on the road. "Yeah, I can tell."

"Where we going now?" she asked.

"To your place. We got another body we gotta take care of."

Asha's heart froze. She hadn't forgotten about the prostitute, but she had pushed the unpleasant memory from her mind.

"Want me to drop you off?" he asked. "I can take care of this by myself."

She swallowed roughly. "No, it's okay. I wanna go."

She was glad for the darkness and the fact that Boom was focused on the dark road. If he could see the look in her eyes, he would've dropped her off for sure.

At her apartment, they found the door unlocked. Asha girded herself for what they might find inside. That didn't help. She couldn't help but gasp at the sight they encountered in the middle of the living room floor. The prostitute lie face down. Her arms were twisted beneath her at angles that would've been uncomfortable if she was among the living. But as Boom had predicted, her soul departed two days ago, probably the moment Ben (or Jerry) interrogated her and determined she wasn't the woman they were looking for.

The smell was bad, but not as bad as Asha expected. Boom said that was because she left her air conditioner on. Even still, the stench was enough to make her gag.

Boom told her, "If you gon' throw up, take it to the restroom. We already got a big enough mess in here."

"No, I'm alright," she managed.

"Go get me a blanket then."

"What are we gonna do, dump her somewhere?"

He shook his head. "Can't do that. No telling how much of your DNA she got on her. I got a place. It'll take some driving, but better safe than sorry."

Asha still didn't know what his plan was, but she went to her bedroom and took the blanket from her bed. She returned to the front room and saw that he had moved some of her furniture around. Boom laid the blanket in the space he cleared and then rolled the woman onto it. The odor suddenly became worse.

Before she could ask, he told her, "Smells always get trapped under a body. I don't know why." Then, "She done got stiff on us. Help me bend her legs."

Asha tried to approach her task with the same objectivity he had, but it was impossible. The woman's death mask was hideous, with one eye fully open, the other half closed. The whites of her eyes were fully crimson, which was indicative of strangulation. That made sense, because she didn't see any bruises on her body, other than a discoloration around her neck.

But it wasn't only the vulgarity that got to her. Asha found it hard to come to terms with the fact that she was partly responsible for this woman's death. Sure, she was a prostitute, an addict and maybe a convict, but she didn't deserve to die this way. Her last moments were filled with fear and violence. Her body lie unattended for two days. If she had children or anyone else who cared about her, they would never know what happened to her or have an opportunity to pay their respects.

Boom saw the tears in her eyes but didn't mention them as they folded the body and wrapped it tightly in the blanket. If he had said something, Asha was prepared to defend herself this time. He could guide her. He could teach her. He could tell her when to pull the trigger. But she'd be damned if he'd tell her not to have feelings.

Before they left the apartment, he said, "I'ma go check the breezeway and the parking lot, to see if there are any cameras."

"There's not," Asha told him.

He said, "I'ma check anyway."

While he was gone, Asha said a quick prayer for the woman. She apologized for bringing her into this and asked God to rest her soul. Asha did not ask for forgiveness for herself, because she knew she wasn't done sinning.

When Boom returned, he tossed her the keys to the Charger. He then bent and hefted the body with hardly any effort.

"We gotta hurry," he said. "Ain't nobody out there now, but you never know. Grab your key off the bar, so you can lock the door. When we get downstairs, I need you to open the trunk for me."

Boom didn't tell her where they were going when they got back on the freeway, but he did say he had a plan for her apartment.

"I got a guy who'll take care of it. He can match the carpet and replace the section she was on. He can redo the whole floor if he has to, without nobody in the office knowing. He real discreet. He can get rid of the smell too."

"I ain't never sleeping in that place again," Asha told him with a shudder. "I don't know if I even want my furniture."

Boom didn't respond to that.

They drove all the way to Alvarado. When Boom got off the freeway, he took a county road for another ten minutes. The street didn't have any streetlights or curbs. An inattentive driver could easily find themselves in a ditch or colliding with a tree. He finally slowed and turned onto a property. Rather than a house, Asha saw a trailer home in the distance. There was nearly an acre of well-maintained land between the trailer and the neighbors on either side. Asha knew Boom had access to a number of residences, but this one surprised her. Maybe this is where he came when he *really* had to lay low.

Boom drove past the trailer home. In the distance, his headlights shone on an old, metal barn that was not in the best shape. The scene reeked of a chainsaw massacre, but with Boom there, Asha wasn't too freaked out.

He came to a stop in front of the barn and left his headlights shining on the large doors.

Before getting out of the car, he told her, "You don't have to come in. I can take care of this."

Asha remained seated. She watched him walk to the barn and unlock it. He went inside, and a dim light came on. He returned to the car, popped the trunk and retrieved the wrapped body. Asha's curiosity got the best of her when he returned to the barn with the bundle in his arms. Her heart kicked so hard, she could feel it pounding in her feet as she exited the car. Other than the moonlight, the night was completely dark. Without street lights, the darkness was all encompassing, as if she was wading through a black sea.

She peeked into the barn and saw something as bad as a chainsaw massacre. Boom was stuffing the body into a large, plastic barrel. Asha's revulsion was magnified when she saw this was one of four identical containers. Two were sealed. The barrels weren't completely transparent, but she saw that there was a dark, soupy substance in them. The fourth container was empty.

Boom briefly looked up at her before returning to his work. After a little pushing from the top, he managed to get the body fully inside the barrel. He then walked to a shelf and picked up a gas mask. Asha's mouth fell open, her eyes as big as quarters. She thought this man had ruined her ability to be shocked by anything he had to offer, but nope. This was now the craziest shit she'd ever witnessed.

Boom secured the gas mask before hefting a large paint bucket. He had half a dozen more lined up against the wall. Boom poured the contents into the barrel, and the body immediately began to smolder. The smoke from whatever chemical he was using rose towards his face in thick plumes. Asha's jaw dropped even further. She looked from the container he was working on back to the other two, understanding they both had what was left of a body in them.

What the fuck...

It took six gallons of hydrofluoric acid to fill the barrel he'd stuffed the prostitute in. Boom put a lid on the container and locked it. Asha remained frozen in place when he returned the gas mask to the counter and walked towards her, turning off the light along the way.

He told her, "Back up, so I can close this door."

Asha almost fell as she stumbled backwards.

When he was done, he said, "You still wanna roll with me tonight, or you want me to drop you off?"

The way he asked made her wonder if the previous owner of the wig she was wearing was currently decomposing in one of those barrels.

She couldn't stop her teeth from chattering when she replied. "I don't want you to drop me off. I'm – I still wanna go with you."

He made a sound that might have been a chuckle before heading to the car.

CHAPTER TWELVE
CORNER BOYS

It was a quiet ride back to the city. Asha had a million questions about the containers in Boom's barn, but she was afraid of the answers he'd give her, so she didn't ask. The gas mask he'd used had a strap on the bottom, so Boom used a comb to straighten and fluff out his beard as he drove. The only thing he said to her before they reached Overbrook Meadows' city limits was, "How does my beard look?" He turned her way for a second.

There wasn't much light in the car, but the lights on the freeway provided enough illumination for her to tell him, "It looks good. You look very handsome."

"Handsome ain't what I'm going for," he replied as he returned the comb to the center console.

She told him, "I know. When people see that beard coming, they know what time it is."

He nodded, glad that she had remembered.

"So where we going now?" she asked.

"To the east side. I'm looking for some corner boys."

"*Corner boys*? Why?"

"You'll see," he said cryptically.

Twenty minutes later, they arrived in a quiet neighborhood that wasn't as quiet as it seemed. It was after one a.m. on a Saturday night. Boom drove through several apartment complexes that were bustling with activity. There were clubgoers returning home tipsy and boisterous. A lot of hoodrats and thugs parking lot pimping. But most noticeably were all the addicts, or *j's*, as Boom described them.

"Why they call them that?" Asha wondered.

"It's short for junkies," he explained. "And where there's j's, there's corner boys. I think this is a good spot."

The complex they were in wasn't as lively as some of the others, but there was still signs of life. As Boom drove though the parking lot, he directed Asha's attention to one of the breezeways. On the ground floor, she saw three young men loitering there. They didn't appear to be doing anything but shooting the shit, but she could tell by their appearance that they were dealers.

"You remember what I told you about the dope game?" Boom asked as he drove to the opposite end of the parking lot.

Asha knew they'd had a conversation about his time as a dealer, but she didn't know what he wanted to hear.

He said, "I told you the dope game is stupid, because you're always exposed, waiting on the laws to run up on you."

Asha nodded. She did remember that.

"But the laws ain't the only ones you gotta worry about," Boom said as he found a parking spot he liked. "You gotta worry about goons running up on you too. We finna rob them boys."

Asha's eyes widened and then registered confusion. "Wha, why?"

"Because this is King David's territory," he told her. "Or at least it was. Whoever took over his organization after I killed him is still running these apartments. Whoever that person is is probably the one who hired Ben and Jerry. We gon' use these dope boys to draw him out."

Asha understood the basics of his plan, but she was confused about the logistics. Boom didn't take the time to explain it further.

"When we run up on 'em," he said, "we'll play it by ear. Don't get too caught up on anything I tell them. But you need to pay attention to what I tell you. I don't plan on shooting none of them, but if shit goes bad, we might have to. You was asking if there was a code word I could use if I wanted you to pull the trigger..."

She nodded, her heart racing.

"I think the one we already used is good enough," Boom said.

She frowned.

"When we were under that underpass, I used your name," he continued. "I said, *Asha*, you need to do this or that..."

She nodded.

"That's your code word," he said. "If I say your name, that means it's time to body these niggas. I would never use your real name unless there's not gonna be a witness left behind to repeat it. You get it?"

She nodded.

"So when we go over there," he quizzed her, "If I say, '*Shoot this nigga*,' what do you do?"

She thought about it and said, "Nothing."

"Naw, I mean, yeah, basically. You don't shoot 'em, but you can put the gun in his face."

She took a deep breath and nodded.

"If I say, '***Asha**, shoot this nigga*,' then what?"

"I shoot him."

"*In the head*," Boom clarified. "We not leaving no witnesses, if it come to that."

She realized they were about to play a deadly game of Simon says.

"You ready?" he asked.

She wasn't, but she nodded.

"Cock your pistol," he instructed, "and take it off safety. Keep your finger out the trigger guard, unless it's time to kill."

They used the cover of darkness and the cars in the parking lot to creep on the unsuspecting dealers. Boom appeared on the left with his shotgun held at the ready. When the boys looked up and saw him, he cocked it for effects. The chambered round sounded deadly, all by itself.

CHA-CHICK!

"You know what it is," his voice boomed. "Hands up. Don't try no shit."

As instructed, Asha ambushed them from the opposite side of the breezeway. Boom didn't give her any opening lines, so she just pointed her gun at them, making sure Boom wasn't in her line of sight.

"Ain't this some shit," the oldest of the group said as he looked from one assailant to the other.

They all raised their hands chest high.

"Drop out," Boom instructed. "Turn them pockets inside out. Shoes too. Take 'em off. I want everything!"

"Man, you fucking, up," the older one said as they complied. He had a black bandana tied around his neck like Bankroll Fresh. His cohorts looked scared shitless.

"Naw, y'all the ones fucking up," Boom told him. "Raise your shirt up. All of y'all." A moment later, he told Asha, "This nigga got a pistol! Bust him!"

Asha trained her gun on Bandana. Her features were as menacing as Boom's when she said, "Nigga, you trying something?"

"Bust that nigga!" Boom said again. "He finna reach!"

"Nigga, I ain't reaching!" Bandana squealed. "You told me to raise my shirt!"

"Get that off him," Boom told Asha. "Wet him, if he make a move."

Bandana mean mugged her as she approached him and removed the pistol from his waistband.

"*Don't be eyeballing my woman!*" Boom barked. He looked down at the drugs and money that had accumulated at their feet. "This ain't all of it," he said knowingly. He swung the shotgun in the direction of the youngest one. "Why you still got yo fucking shoes on?"

The youngster kicked them off frantically, his hands still raised. "*I'm sorry, man! Here!*"

Boom looked past them to the door they were standing in front of. It was partly open.

"Who in there?" he asked the youngster.

"*Nobody!*"

"Come on," he said, heading that way. "You go first. Keep yo fucking hands up!"

The youngster walked into the apartment with Boom on his tail. Before he went inside, Boom told Asha, "If either of these motherfuckers so much as sneeze, pop both of 'em."

Asha tried not to show how freaked out she was. Boom never said anything about leaving her alone during the robbery. And he didn't use her name with the last command. She realized she'd have to make an executive decision, if they tried something while he was gone. She prayed it wouldn't come to that.

While he was inside, Bandana continued to mean mug her.

"Bitch, you know who y'all fucking with?" he asked.

"I know you about to be a dead man, if you don't shut your fucking mouth," she growled. "Try me, nigga. I'll show you how a bitch get down. Say one more thing. *Say one more goddamn thing*!"

Bandana grimaced as he swallowed his words and his pride.

Thankfully Boom and the youngster weren't inside for very long. When they returned, Boom toted a pillowcase with something inside. "Jackpot," he said to Asha. "Get back on the wall," he told the youngster.

"You bet not have gave him that shit," Bandana told Youngster.

"*He was gon' shoot me*," Youngster whined.

"You a stupid motherfucker," Bandana told him.

Boom shoved the pillowcase in Youngster's chest. "Get all this shit off the ground and put it in there."

The boy bent and did as he was told.

Boom approached the leader, his features hard and menacing. "You talking a lot of shit."

Bandana didn't back down. "You know whose shit you fucking with?"

"I know this used to be King David's block, but that ugly motherfucker dead. I don't know who you working for now."

"Don't be talking shit about KD."

Asha couldn't believe the boy's gall. He may have been an idiot, but he was a true soldier.

"What you gon' do about it?" Boom asked him. "That nigga been dead for damn near three months, and y'all ain't did shit."

"We gon' find out who did it," Bandana said.

Asha was surprised to see tears in his eyes.

"We gon' find out." He struggled to maintain composure. "We is."

Boom backed away from him and grabbed the bag from Youngster when he was done filling it. "All of y'all get on your knees. Face the wall. Hands behind your head. Lock your fingers."

He waited while the dealers grudgingly complied.

"Y'all stay like that for thirty seconds," Boom said as he backed away. "Come on," he told Asha.

She kept her gun trained on them as she moved in his direction.

"*Count out loud*!" Boom demanded. "I wanna hear that shit."

The youngster started counting as Boom and Asha disappeared around the corner and into the night.

Asha's heart was still thumping when they got back to the car. Boom told her to get in the back seat, while he got behind the wheel. She thought he'd flee the scene, but he simply started the car and remained in the spot.

"What's happening?" she breathed.

"Nothing," he said as he casually removed his beard and ball cap. "We gon' wait."

"Wait? *Right here*?"

"They don't know what we driving, and as long as you stay back there, I'm not the person that robbed them. I'm just some dude sitting in a car. I ain't even got no beard," he said as he placed it on the passenger seat.

Asha thought he was crazy, but so far, he was always a step ahead of his opponents.

"Take your wig off," he said. "And those necklaces."

"What about this mole?"

"Yeah, take that off too."

"Thank God," she said as she plucked it from her nose.

When they had both removed their disguises, Boom left the parking spot, but he didn't go far. He circled the lot and came to a stop facing the breezeway. They were about forty yards away, but Asha worried that was too close.

"What are you doing now?" she asked, her eyes wide.

"We gon' wait for them to call their boss. I took all their dope and their guns, so he'll have to come and give them all that back."

"You don't think this is too close?"

156

"How else I'ma see him when he comes?"

"Damn, Boom. If they come outside, they can see us."

"Remember when we talked about human nature?"

Asha remembered that conversation, and she was sure there wasn't any mention of what was happening right now.

"You gotta know how your enemies think," Boom said. "If somebody robs you, what you think they'll do next?"

Asha thought about it and said, "Take off?"

"Right. Would you ever think they'd sit there and watch you?"

She shook her head, understanding what he was getting at.

"Another thing is," Boom said, "people don't watch their surroundings like you think, especially if they don't suspect anything. When was the last time you went to the store and looked around the parking lot before you got back in your car, to make sure no one was watching you?"

She shook her head. "Never."

He nodded. "Even if I'm wrong about all that, we done took off our disguises, so I'm just some random dude sitting in a car, as long as they don't see you."

Asha took that as her cue to sit back and shut up.

They waited for about thirty minutes, before everything Boom said would happen came to be. The dope boys remained inside the apartment the whole time. A dozen customers came to visit them, and they were all turned away.

While they waited, Boom said, "Did you hear how they don't know who killed KD?"

"Yeah. That's a good thing?"

He nodded. "If they don't even know Big Hooch did it, then they definitely don't know about me. That cuts down on the people I have to silence. I'm hoping Ben and Jerry only told the person that hired them."

Asha hoped so too.

"You did good," he told her.

"Really?"

"Yeah. You did everything I needed you to."

She smiled. "Once again, it looks like you needed me, just like in the underpass."

"How you figure?"

"I had to watch the bigger two, when you took the other one in the apartment."

"I could've did that on my own. I would've made all of 'em come with me."

"You just can't admit that you like having me around..."

Boom did not confirm or deny her assessment.

Five minutes later, he announced, "I think that's him," when a champagne colored Escalade pulled into the parking lot and came to a stop in front of the breezeway. Asha watched the scene from the backseat.

The Escalade sat there for a few seconds, and then all three dealers came out and crowded around it. Bandana went to the driver's side. After a brief conversation, the driver handed him a duffle bag through the window. The stranger pulled away, and the dealers returned to the apartment.

"That's the guy we're looking for?" Asha asked.

"Maybe," Boom said as he rolled out of his parking spot. "We gotta follow him to find out."

They followed the Escalade through the dark streets for fifteen minutes. Boom kept a respectable distance but never lost sight of it at a traffic light or stop sign. He gave the SUV a little more leeway when it turned into a middle-class neighborhood. He waited at the corner when the truck pulled into a driveway. He was grateful the driver didn't disappear inside the garage. Boom drove slowly past as a man exited the vehicle and headed for the front door of a nice home.

"Damn," he muttered.

"What's wrong?" Asha asked.

"That's not the man I'm looking for," Boom told her as they slowed at the next corner. He made a right and circled the block, approaching the house from the same direction as before. This time he stopped a few houses down and put the car in park. He killed the engine.

"You can come sit up front," he said to Asha.

She exited the vehicle and got in on the passenger side.

"How do you know that's not who you're looking for?" she asked him.

"Because I know King David has a brother named Solomon. That's who I thought I was following, but it wasn't him."

"David and Solomon? Their mother named them after biblical kings?"

Boom nodded. "Maybe she thought they'd be pastors. Instead, they grew up to be dope boys."

"Do they call the other one *King* Solomon?"

Boom shook his head. "Naw. I don't think so."

"So who's this guy?" Asha asked, looking at the house where the Escalade was parked.

"I don't know. Probably a lieutenant. It's a pretty big organization."

"Okay. What do we do now?"

"I gotta sit on this car. Hopefully tomorrow he'll go see Solomon."

"We gonna wait here all night?"

He nodded. "You need to go to the bathroom or something? I got a Gatorade bottle back there for me, but I don't know if that would work for you."

"No, it won't," she said, smiling. "But I think I'm okay."

"You *think*? It's two o'clock. He may not move again until the sun comes up."

"I guess I should probably go to the bathroom then," she decided.

He started the car and they took off again.

He took them to the Waffle House and ordered two meals to-go while Asha used the restroom. Boom decided to go himself while they waited for the food.

They returned to the house and saw the Escalade hadn't moved.

"I doubt if he's going anywhere tonight," Boom said as they ate.

"You wanna come back in the morning?"

He shook his head. "That's not the way stakeouts work. The dope game doesn't have regular hours. Shit could pop off at any minute. We gotta be ready."

They ate quietly for a while, and then Asha asked, "Are you gonna kill Solomon, if he's the one who hired Ben and Jerry?"

Boom nodded. "That's the plan."

"I'm not trying to talk you out of it, but do you think that's fair? You kill his brother, and he tries to avenge him. Then you come back and kill him too..."

"I never said it was fair. It's a him or me situation at this point, and I'll be damned if I chose somebody else over me."

Asha quieted down again and finished her dinner. Boom didn't speak either while he ate.

An hour later, it was 3:30am. Boom had told her not to use her phone. He didn't want the glow from the electronic to alert anyone to their presence. Without her iPhone, Asha didn't know what she was supposed to do with all this time. Boom seemed content to stare at the house.

"This is boring," she complained. "Stakeouts are boring."

"I never said it would be fun," he replied with a chuckle. "You can get in the backseat and take a nap."

"Are you gonna come back there with me?" she asked, her naughty grin on full flare.

"Uh-uhn. One of us gotta keep his head in the game."

"Speaking of head..."

She reached into his lap and unfastened his pants. He didn't object when she unzipped them and pulled his dick out. When he didn't stop her from stroking him, she went in for the kill. She leaned over and sucked his dick like she was getting paid for it. The sounds of her slurping filled the car. It was soon joined by Boom's grunts of pleasure. The feel of his rock-hard meat in her mouth made her wet, but she knew he'd draw the line if she tried to straddle him.

He reached to stop her after a few minutes. She looked up at him, her lips full and moist.

She asked, "What's wrong?"

His big chest rose and fell. "You finna make a mess," he managed.

"How I'ma make a mess?" she asked, her eyes low and sultry.

"'Cause I'm finna cum."

"I promise not to make a mess."

He stared into her eyes. His widened slightly, as the meaning of her words hit him.

She ducked her head again and picked up where she left off. After a minute he reached for her again, but he palmed the back of her head this time and directed her to take him in deeper. Asha hummed her approval around his dick.

She felt his legs stiffen a moment before he exploded in her mouth. The taste of his salty sweetness made her mouth water. She swallowed it down and kept stroking and sucking, milking every last drop from him. His grip on the back of her head tightened with each spasm, until they finally subsided, and his head fell back on the headrest. She backed away and saw that his mouth hung open, his eyes half closed. It took a bit of gentleness to get his dick back in his pants and leave everything the way she had found it, but she managed.

She sat back in her seat and sighed, smiling. "I guess stakeouts aren't so bad," she said, her eyes back on the house.

"I ain't never had one like this," Boom replied. "I don't think I can go back to doing it the regular way."

"You like having me around, don't you?"

He frowned. "I ain't say all that."

She shook her head, giggling.

CHAPTER THIRTEEN
DADDY TIME

The next morning, Asha was awakened to movement. Last night, she'd taken Boom up on his offer to nap in the back seat, but she didn't realize she was sleeping so soundly. She looked up and saw that the sun had risen, and the Charger was once again on the move. She recognized they were still in the neighborhood they staked out last night. Ahead of them, she saw the champagne colored Escalade stop at the corner before turning right. Boom stopped at the same corner and waited a few beats before making the same turn.

He looked up at her in the rearview mirror and said, "We got some action."

"What time is it?" Asha asked as she rubbed her tired eyes.

"About nine-thirty," he replied. "I thought we were gonna have to abandon our watch, because one of the neighbors up the street left for church a few minutes ago. If more people started to move around, we wouldn't have been able to sit there in broad daylight. But our guy was the next to leave."

"You been up the whole time?"

He nodded.

"You not tired?"

"Not right now. I was before he came out, but now I'm wide awake. "

Now that he mentioned it, Asha felt a boost of adrenaline as well. She couldn't wait for this to be over, but she couldn't deny that Boom had her on a nonstop thrill ride.

They followed the Escalade for an hour and a half. Boom had to be careful when the first stop was an apartment complex. From a distance, they saw the driver park in a fire lane and wait for a couple of minutes before someone came to the car and handed him a duffle bag. The Escalade repeated this process over a dozen times, mostly at apartments, but also in the projects and dope houses.

"This is when it gets tricky," he told Asha after the second pickup.

"How come?"

"Following him on the streets is hard enough. But when he goes in these apartments, it's easier for him to spot me if he sees the same car at every complex. Plus it looks like he's doing his morning pickups, so he should be on high alert. Did you see at that first stop he scooped up two goons to roll with him?"

"Yeah, I saw that."

"That's his backup," Boom informed her, "to make sure he don't get robbed."

"Why don't you hang back and wait till he gets ready to leave the apartments, before you get back on his tail?"

"Because I don't know where his last stop is," Boom told her. "If I assume he's about to do another pickup, but he goes into one of these places to give everything to Solomon —

or whoever is in charge – I'll miss my opportunity. I'll have to stakeout that house again and start over."

Asha understood his conundrum.

"Only thing we can hope for," Boom continued, "is they more worried about somebody trying something when they parked and not what's happening when they on the road."

Asha hoped his calculations were correct.

Once again, Boom pulled off what she would've considered impossible. After the last pick up, The Escalade got on the freeway, headed north. Boom relaxed, finding it easier to tail him then. They followed the SUV all the way to a Fossil Creek neighborhood, where the average home cost half a million.

"This gotta be it," Boom muttered, mostly to himself. "Solomon raking in all that money in the hood and living high on the hog."

Asha agreed. She stared out the window like a tourist. The only person she knew personally who could afford to live in this area was her boss Mr. Luck, who was a millionaire many times over.

Boom hung back when the Escalade turned into a driveway large enough to fit six cars. He wasn't disappointed when the garage door rolled open, and the SUV dipped inside. Once the door closed, Boom continued down the street and made a few turns, until he was leaving the neighborhood.

"I think I'm in the wrong profession," he mused.

Asha didn't disagree with that assertion, but she asked, "Why you say that?"

"How much money you think they picked up this morning?"

She had no idea. "Forty, fifty thousand?"

"That would be four thousand at each spot," he calculated. "I'm thinking it's more than that. But even if it is only fifty, that's from one night. If I was to start robbing these cats when they do they morning pickups..."

Asha frowned. "I think your job is already dangerous enough."

"I'm just saying."

"Why are we leaving? I thought you said that's where Solomon lives."

"I'm pretty sure it is. But we don't have to wait for him now. He got all them niggas in there anyway. We'll come back and catch him when he's by hisself. You ain't ready to take a break? I know you need a nap."

"I could use some sleep. I'm sure you need some more than me."

"Yeah," he said. "Tonight might be another long night. We should get some rest."

They stopped at Whataburger for breakfast and ate it on the way to Boom's home. When he pulled into the garage, Asha was grateful that it didn't smell as bad as the last time they were there. But the lingering scent of death brought back a lot of memories, mostly about the ghastly goo in those huge containers.

They showered and slept together. Asha wasn't sure why this man made her so horny, but she couldn't keep her hands out of his boxers. His dick responded to her advances, but she heard him snoring lightly and subdued her animalistic urges.

Boom woke her up at five p.m. She wasn't sure how he always managed to slip out of bed without her realizing it. He was already dressed in jeans and a white tee. His disguise for the night featured a moustache/goatee combo and a high-top haircut with short dreads that were bleached, leaving them frizzy and orange-tinted. So far, Asha liked all of his disguises, but this one made him look really sexy.

She wondered if no one was getting killed tonight, since he didn't opt for the infamous beard. She doubted if she'd be so lucky.

"I need you to wear this dress tonight," he told her. "It's about your size."

Asha noticed the garment was laid out on the bed. It was black with spaghetti straps. It appeared to be form-fitting. She didn't bother mentioning that dresses weren't her thing, because his statement sounded non-negotiable.

He stepped into the closet and returned with another wig. This one was short and curly with auburn highlights.

"You need to put this on too," he said. "And I'ma give you some glasses and a nose ring. It's a clip-on, but it looks real. We need to stop and get some lipstick and some shoes to match that dress."

Asha tried to subdue a sudden surge of apprehension. She badly wanted to know where the dress and women's wigs had come from. But she had come to learn that Boom was sometimes approachable and other times not. This didn't appear to be one of those times when he would put up with her personal questions.

"Okay," was her only response.

They stopped at Walmart for the lipstick and DSW for the shoes. Boom waited in the car both times. At the shoe store, Asha asked him, "Is it okay if I get sandals? I don't like heels or wedges."

He told her, "Yeah, but you should rethink your stance on dressing sexy. You look good in that dress."

Asha's chest and face heated. That was the first time he'd ever complimented her appearance. But it wasn't enough to change her mind about her shoe selection. She bought a pair of stylish sandals and wore them out of the store. Boom nodded his approval when she got back in the car.

They returned to the Fossil Creek neighborhood and found it active as the sun began to set. Boom shook his head when he turned onto the street the Escalade had led them to.

"This might not work," he said. "A neighborhood like this, I can't sit in front of somebody's house for a few hours. They gon' think we trying to rob them."

"What should we do?" Asha asked as Solomon's house came into view up ahead.

"I think I'ma have to ring his ass."

She looked over at him, confused.

"I'll show you."

He passed the house and drove deeper into the neighborhood, until they encountered a park with a looping trail and a huge duck pond. The area was crowded with joggers, bikers and whole families. Boom pulled into the parking lot and told Asha, "Wait here," as he exited the vehicle. He removed something from the trunk of the car and got back behind the wheel. She saw that he had two Ring doorbells.

"I can plant these near the house," he explained. He removed two cellphones from the center console. "I don't like using them, because if someone sees it, they can take it or report it. With all these motherfuckers out here jogging and walking their dogs, it'll be hard to even put 'em where I want 'em. White people nosey as hell. But I think it's our best bet."

Asha shook her head in wonderment. There seemed to be no limit to this man's cunning.

The doorbell devices were already registered to the cellphones. He turned them on and had Asha hold them with the cameras facing out of her window, while he viewed the live stream.

He liked what he saw, but she wondered, "How are these even working? Don't they need Wi-Fi?"

He told her, "I got a mobile hotpot in this car. But the range is only 150 feet."

"So you still have to be parked close to them?"

He nodded. "The last time I used them, I put one on each corner and then left my car in the middle. I took off on foot, like I was going for a walk. People don't get suspicious about an empty car in front of their house."

"That's smart."

"Yeah, but I can't do that today, with you dressed like that."

"Um, you picked my whole outfit."

"We'll figure something out," he said with a grin.

He returned to Solomon's house and picked a stop sign where he could tape the first camera. Before he got out of the car, Asha saw that the gods of death always seemed to show him favor.

"Wait," she said, staring at the house. "Somebody's leaving."

Boom looked and grinned when he saw a Mercedes backing out of the garage. There was a Lexus parked next to it with a personalized plate that read, "Ms Thang." He assumed the Lexus belonged to the woman of the house, and the Benz was driven by Solomon.

"This gotta be my lucky day," he said as the Mercedes backed into the street and then began to head their way. "*Duck down*," Boom instructed, when he realized the car was about to drive right by them.

Asha couldn't lean all the way forward, she went sideways, resting her head in his lap. Boom pretended to look down at his phone as the car passed, but his keen eyes caught everything.

"Alright," he said.

Asha sat up, and he put the Charger in drive. He performed a U-turn and began to follow his target.

"Was that him?" she asked.

"Yup. That's Solomon."

Boom was focused again. She could see murder in his eyes. She took a deep, slow breath, but it didn't calm her nerves.

"He got a kid in the car," Boom informed her. "A little girl. She don't look no older than four or five."

Asha's eyes widened. Boom looked over at her, his features hard.

She couldn't help but voice her dissent. "I don't wanna do nothing to him, if he got his kid with him."

"I know you don't," Boom said, his eyes back on the road. "But you ain't me. And it's too late to drop yo ass off."

They followed Solomon out of the neighborhood to a nearby McDonalds. Boom sped up when he saw him about to turn into the parking lot. He wanted to catch him before he entered the restaurant, rather than wait on him to leave. He pulled into a parking spot directly behind the target and reached over Asha's lap to grab a pistol from the glove compartment. If he noticed her look of dread, he didn't comment on it. The only instruction he had for her this time was, "Come on."

She exited the car with him and watched as he accosted Solomon when he got out of the Mercedes. Boom flashed his gun but didn't feel the need to point it at him. Solomon was freaked out enough. They had caught him slipping to the fullest.

"Go get in on the passenger side," Boom ordered. "Baby," he said to Asha, "You get in back, keep that little girl company."

Asha's heart dropped to the pit of her stomach. Her face broke out in a cold sweat. She couldn't move.

"Nigga, you didn't hear what I said?"

For a moment, Asha thought Boom was talking to her, but Solomon hadn't moved either.

"*Man, what the fuck y'all doing? I ain't got no money,*" Solomon pleaded. He looked from Boom to Asha, his eyes sick with terror. "*What y'all want? I'm with my dauyhter.*"

Asha thought the man was handsome, even in his state of distress. He wore a full beard, shaved low. His hair was short, his skin caramel. He wore canvas shorts with a tee-shirt and flip flops. He was completely unprepared for the drama that was about to ensue.

"I'ma say this one more time..." Boom's voice was conversational, but his eyes were anything but. "Get yo bitch ass in on the passenger side. My girl gon' get in the back with yo daughter. You try to stop her or talk back again, and the little girl is gon' be the first one I kill."

Asha couldn't stop her jaw from dropping. She and Solomon wore the same expression.

"*A'ight, man, chill. Please don't do nothing to my daughter. Whatever you want, I can get it for you. Just, just...*" His eyes widened when he realized he was talking and not moving.

He stepped out of Boom's way and walked to the other side of the car on stiff legs. He and Asha came within a foot of each other on the passenger side. When they locked eyes, his were pleading. She wanted hers to be menacing, but she knew she didn't pull it off. They both got in the car. Asha immediately looked to the little girl, who wasn't as shocked as she should've been.

"Daddy? Who are these people?" The princess was caramel colored, like her father. She was rocking a frizzy 'fro and the cutest, little sun dress.

Asha was so disgusted with herself, she nearly vomited.

"*Alright, alright,*" Solomon said. He turned Boom's way and held his hands up. All ten fingers were trembling. "Wha, what is it y'all want? I don't know y'all. I didn't do nothing."

"Close yo door" Boom told him. He looked back at Asha. "Baby, you close yours too."

"*Please don't hurt my baby,*" Solomon cried as he closed the door.

Asha couldn't see his face at that moment, but judging by the quality of his voice, she knew his eyes were filled with tears. She closed her door as well.

"Nigga, you acting like a bitch right about now," Boom told him. "How you running all them niggas in the hood, and you sitting up here finna cry? Do them niggas even respect you?"

Solomon's chest shuddered. "Oh, oh, okay. So, so you know me? This got something to do with my business?"

"Yeah, I know you," Boom said.

"Alright, okay, so, so what you want? You want money? You know I got it. I can, I can–"

"*Daddy.*"

"It's okay, baby," Solomon said, turning to look at her. "These are just some of Daddy's friends. We'll be done in a minute."

"I want ice cream," the girl said. "Aren't we getting ice cream?"

"Yeah, we are. Just, just give Daddy a second..." He returned his attention to the gunman. "This is about money?"

Boom shook his head. "Naw. This about your brother."

Confused, Solomon said, "My, my brother? KD, he, he dead."

"I know," Boom said. "I'm trying to find out who killed him."

The confusion worked its way to Solomon's whole face. "You – you think I had something to do with my brother getting killed?"

"Naw. I wanna know what you know about it."

"Man, I don't – I don't get this shit. If you trying to figure out who killed my brother, why you coming at me like this – doing this shit in front of my daughter?"

"I think you do know who killed your brother," Boom said. "I think you lying to me right now. You wanna change some of your answers, or we gotta take this a step further."

"Man, I don't know who killed him! I swear!"

Boom looked to the backseat. "Baby."

"Yeah," Asha said.

"Why don't you take that little girl to get some ice cream. But not here. They got some *way* better ice cream in our neighborhood. I'll meet up with y'all later."

"What?" Solomon nearly shit his drawers. *"Say, man, don't do that!"* He turned all the way in his seat and pleaded with Asha directly. *"Don't touch her!"*

"Come on," Asha said to the girl, ignoring him. She reached and unfastened the little angel's seatbelt. "I'ma take you to get some ice cream at a way better place."

The girl's eyes filled with tears. She told her father, *"Daddy, I wanna go home."*

Asha hated herself for playing this role. But Boom didn't use her name when he gave the instruction, so she knew he didn't really want her to take the girl. Still... She didn't think God would ever forgive her for harming this child, even if it was psychological rather than physical harm.

"*Okay, okay, okay,*" Solomon stammered. "Big Hooch. He the one who killed KD. Alright? That's all I know. Please, y'all leave my baby out of this."

Boom continued his interrogation, as if no one in the car was having a mental breakdown.

"You hired somebody to kill Big Hooch?"

"*No. I didn't.*"

"Why not?"

"*What, I, I just didn't!*"

"That don't make no sense. A man kill your brother, and you not gon' do shit about it?"

"That revenge shit brings drama," Solomon said. "That was KD's game. All that murder shit. I'm about my money. Killing a nigga ain't gon' put a dime in my pocket, and I'll probably start losing money when they retaliate. That bullshit, gangbanging, take one of mine, we take one of yours shit ain't never been for me. Big Hooch dead anyway, so I didn't have to get involved."

Asha was surprised by how the stress had made him reveal his true character. This was the Solomon Boom wanted to question all along.

"Somebody in your organization had Hooch killed?" Boom asked.

"Naw," Solomon said, shaking his head. "Wouldn't nobody on my team make a move like that without it going through me first."

"Look me in my eyes and tell me you didn't hire nobody to go after Big Hooch."

Solomon looked Boom dead in the eyes. "I swear on my mama and my daughter: I didn't hire nobody to go after Big Hooch."

Boom nodded. "Alright. Well tell me who else would've did it."

"Man, I don't know."

"KD have any kids?"

"He got a son. He 18. He wouldn't have done that, though – couldn't have, even if he wanted to."

"Why not?"

"He ain't got enough paper to hire no killer."

"Where can I find him?"

Solomon gave him a name and address.

"What about y'all daddy? You don't think he'd want to go after the man who killed his son?"

"Me and KD got different dads. Mine dead, and his just got out the joint. He ain't got the means to do that either."

"Gimme his info anyway."

Solomon gave up the information without hesitation.

Boom shook his head in disappointment. "Why would you give up your nephew and KD's father like that? Far as you know, I'm finna go kill both them niggas."

"I'd put my daughter's life in front of theirs any day," Solomon said. "I love my nephew, but I love my daughter more. And me and KD's dad ain't even that close. Fuck that nigga."

Boom watched him for a few seconds before saying, "A'ight, Solomon. Me and baby 'bout to get out the car. If you thinking about grabbing yo strap and taking a shot at us before we take off, you better hope you hit both of us in the head. 'Cause we gon' bust back, and, like I told you, I'ma try to kill yo little girl first."

"I ain't gon' fuck with y'all," Solomon promised. "Just leave me and mines out of whatever the fuck y'all got going on."

CHAPTER FOURTEEN
HAVE A HEART

"You got something to say," Boom asked as they left the restaurant.

Asha shook her head without looking his way.

"If it's something on your chest, you might as well get it off," he said. "Ain't no sense in sitting there with yo face all scrunched up."

She looked at him then. "I think that was wrong."

He shrugged. "Yeah, I'm sure it was."

"But you don't care." That was more a statement than a question.

"Pretty much everything I do is wrong. Was that more wrong than blowing somebody's brains out?"

"That's different."

"How?"

"'Cause that little girl didn't have nothing to do with it. You don't have a problem involving somebody's kid?"

"Nope. Kids are great for leverage. That man told me everything I wanted to know."

She sighed, her nostrils flaring.

"You know what," he said, "I'm sick of you acting like you don't know who and what you're dealing with. You know what I do for a living. You saw what was in those barrels. And now you seen the way I handled that man in front of his daughter. If you still don't know I'm a motherfucking monster, then you just don't wanna see it.

"Now, I'ma ask you this one mo' time: Do you want me to drop you off somewhere? 'Cause I'm gon' see this through to the end, but you can go stay with your sister or wherever else you want. Ain't nobody gunning for you."

Asha didn't consider the question for as long as she probably should have.

"No. I don't want you to drop me off. I wanna see this through just like you."

"Then stop second-guessing me, 'cause that type of shit makes me think you won't have my back, if it come down to it."

He hadn't looked at her with that mean gaze since the first time they met.

Asha cowered under the glare and said, "Okay. I'm sorry." They were quiet for a minute before she asked, "Did you believe him?"

"Huh?"

"Solomon. Do you believe what he said?"

"Oh, yeah. I believe he didn't hire Ben and Jerry. You don't?"

"I do. I was just wondering how you felt, since you made him look you in the eyes. I figured you had some way to know if he was lying."

"I feel like I have a built-in lie detector," Boom said. "It ain't a hundred percent accurate, but damn near."

Asha had always wondered about that. She thought about the lie she had told him when—

"Like with you," he said, cutting off her thoughts.

What the hell? Is this nigga a mind reader too?

"When my safe house got shot up," Boom said, "I asked if you told anyone where you were going that night. You told me no, but I know that was a lie."

She stared at him, unwilling to confirm or deny that.

"I didn't confront you at the time," he said, "because I wanted to see how it would play out. Once I found out that whoever you told didn't have nothing to do with the shooting, I let it go. But moving forward, don't think you can look me in the eyes and lie to me. And if you *can't* look me in the eyes when you tell me something, I know for sure you're lying."

"That, that's kinda messed up," Asha decided.

"Why?"

"'Cause a woman's got to have some secrets."

"I ain't worried about a white lie, like if you like a dress I picked out for you. I'm talking about big ones, the kind that could get a nigga killed."

She realized Boom was in one of his moods where he might be receptive to questions. Since he was the one who brought up the dress, she figured this was a good time to inquire about it.

"Why do you have women's wigs and clothing? You said you didn't have a woman..."

He looked her way for a second, before his eyes returned to the road. "You asking out of jealousy or curiosity?"

Even though they'd been intimate a couple of times, Asha knew he didn't consider them to be in a relationship. "I don't have no reason to be jealous. I know you ain't my man. But none of the stuff you want me to wear is new. I wanna know who it belongs to."

181

"I had a partner," Boom revealed. "For a while, it was good to have her around. Sometimes a female can open doors I can't. We ran together for about a year."

Asha already knew the answer to her next question. Boom and death went together like peanut butter and jelly. She waited, thinking he'd volunteer the information. But he remained quiet and forced her to ask.

"What happened to her?"

"She had a heart," he said. "I put her in a position where she needed to pull the trigger. She hesitated. It cost her her life."

Asha recognized that Boom partly took responsibility for his former partner's death. But ultimately, he placed the blame on her. She also knew that he was taking a shot at her, because she too had a heart.

She wanted to ask if the woman was also his lover, but that question was rooted in jealousy, so she bit her tongue. She also didn't ask follow up questions about the details of her death. But she did plan to put her foot down in regard to wearing the dead woman's clothing. She didn't ever want Boom to look at her and see another woman.

Plus, Asha was superstitious. Wearing a dead woman's clothes had to be bad luck.

KD's only child was named Cole. In keeping with his father's reverence, he sometimes went by King Cole or KC. Given KD's wealth and reputation, Boom expected the boy to have a lifestyle that was comparable to his uncle's, but the address Solomon gave them led them to a poor neighborhood on the west side.

The sun had begun to set by the time they reached their destination. As Boom drove past KC's house, he saw a late model car in the driveway that had two flat tires. The grass was a little overgrown with bare spots. The house wasn't large enough to have more than three bedrooms. It was in need of a paint job and several other obvious repairs.

"This is a damn shame," Boom said.

Asha asked, "What you mean?"

"This nigga's father was hood rich. I can't believe Solomon ain't putting *nothing* in his nephew's pocket. He ain't gotta buy him a house in his neighborhood, but he shouldn't be cool with his people living like this."

Asha nodded and then asked, "What's the plan?"

"I don't wanna knock on the door," Boom said. "Solomon may have gave him a heads up. Nigga could be waiting on us."

"No, I mean once we find him. Do you just wanna question him or..."

Boom shook his head slightly. "I don't wanna kill this boy. But you already know what the deal is, if he knows I'm the one who took out his father. From the looks of it, though, I think Solomon was right about this kid not having the means. If KC had enough money to hire Ben and Jerry, he wouldn't be living here."

Asha was relieved to hear that, but she knew Boom wouldn't let it go until he was positive.

He surveyed the neighborhood before pulling up to a washateria. Asha looked around, wondering why he had stopped. There were a few ghetto youths milling about but nothing that would indicate KC was among them.

"You see that store across the street," he asked.

Asha followed his eyes and saw a typical hood corner store. Adverts on the windows indicated there was a grill inside. Customers could get anything, from lottery tickets, burgers, chips and cheap wine; basically everything needed to sustain a poverty lifestyle. Asha saw a few more people hanging out in front of the store.

"Yeah," she said. "What about it?"

"I need you to go over there and ask about KC. See if any of them know where he at. Try to find out what he wearing. Act like you his girlfriend or something."

Asha didn't have a problem playing this role. It was a lot better than threatening a five-year-old. "Is this why you wanted me to wear a dress?"

"I didn't know we would end up here when I told you to wear a dress," Boom replied. "But I figured your sexuality might come into play at some point."

She nodded before getting out of the car. The guys Boom wanted her to question looked her way as she crossed the street. She watched them size her up. She did the same to them. She thought they ranged from 17 to 21 years old. They didn't appear to be outwardly dangerous, but there was always a propensity for violence in neighborhoods like this. She was unarmed, but with Boom watching her, she felt no fear.

"What's up, shorty?" one of them said when she drew near.

"What's up?" Asha replied.

"You looking for something?"

"Where you from?" another asked.

She told him, "The south side."

"What you doing over here?"

"Looking for this dude I met the other night," she said. "He go by KC."

"What you looking for him for?" the first one asked with a grin. "That nigga scammed you?"

"Naw," Asha said. "That nigga fucked me, and now he acting like his phone don't work."

They all laughed.

"Like I said, that nigga scammed you," the first one said. "Either he gon' get you for some money or some pussy. Either way, yo ass got scammed." He laughed again.

"Well, he gon' have to look me in the face and tell me he don't want this pussy no more," Asha said. "Y'all know where he at?"

"He over there hooping on Ashford," another one said. "But why you wanna run over there *throwing* the pussy at a nigga?"

"If you wanna throw some pussy, you can throw it over here," the first one said. "I'd call yo fine ass back."

"Me, too," another one said.

"What's yo name?" the first one asked.

Asha ignored him and asked, "Y'all know what he wearing?"

"I seen that nigga, but I don't remember what he wearing," one of them said.

"Shit, me neither," the first one said.

"A'ight, 'preciate y'all," Asha said before turning and walking away.

She crossed the street and got back in the car with Boom. She told him, "He playing ball on Ashford. You know where that is?"

Boom nodded. "They know what he wearing?"

She shook her head.

"Was they suspicious?" he asked.

"No, but they think I'm a stalker."

Boom laughed. "Yeah, I can see that."

Asha frowned, not sure what to make of that comment.

There was a small park on the corner of Ashford and Connecticut. Compared to the park they visited in Fossil Creek, this one could be considered a travesty. Asha couldn't remember the last time she'd seen such a stark contrast between the haves and have nots.

Even with limited daylight, there were over a dozen young men sweating it out on the basketball court. Boom parked and watched the action for a few minutes. He had his windows rolled up, but they could hear all of the cursing and trash talking that had been known to turn a friendly competition into a deadly shooting, especially when there were members of the opposite sex around to push the players' testosterone to dangerous levels.

Boom spotted a crowd of hood rats walking near the court and instructed Asha to repeat her assignment.

"You might have to be a little discreet this time," he told her. "If KC's out there, I don't want them to call him over to you. If they do, just play it off and tell him you were looking for somebody else."

Asha was skeptical. "Tell him I'm looking for a *different* KC?"

He shrugged. "I don't know. Make something up."

She frowned as she got out of the car and made her way to the court. Boom watched her, enjoying the way the game nearly came to a standstill as she strode by. He wondered if Asha was aware of how sexy she was. A few of the girls gave her the stank face when she approached them, but one of them was helpful. She turned and pointed up the street. Boom looked that way and saw a tall, lanky teen four blocks away. The boy was walking away from them, with a basketball in hand, propped on his hip.

Boom's heart rate increased. It was hard to wait for Asha to return before he gave chase. The moment she got back in the car, he went after the boy, who had turned on one of the corners and was out of sight.

"They said that was him up there?" he asked.

"Yeah, in the blue shirt."

When Boom got to the corner he thought the boy turned on, he slowly pulled into the intersection. Sure enough, KC was less than a block ahead of them. The teen looked back and locked eyes with both occupants of the Charger. He looked away and continued on his way. He looked back again when Boom turned on the same street. Boom pulled alongside him and rolled his window down.

He said, "KC," and that was all it took.

The boy bolted like he owed them money.

"Motherfucker," Boom growled. He put the car in park and hurriedly unfastened his seatbelt.

KC abandoned his basketball before zipping into an alley and out of sight.

Before hopping out of the Charger, Boom told Asha, "Pull around the corner and cut him off."

Asha had no idea what she was supposed to do when KC emerged on the other side, but Boom was running full speed by then, and she didn't have a chance to ask.

The teenager was quick. He had youth on his side and homefield advantage. Rather than the paved alleyways they had in better neighborhoods, this alley was overgrown with grass, shrubbery, and of course illegal dumping.

But what Boom lacked in youth, he made up for with speed and determination. He easily caught up with the boy and tackled him from behind. Their bodies rolled on the rough earth. KC initially ended up on top. Before he could mount an offensive, Boom flipped him over and pinned him down with a knee on his shoulder. He restrained the teen's free arm with one hand and grabbed his throat with the other.

"Stop fighting!"

The boy continued to struggle mightily. Boom began to squeeze his throat, until KC's eyes bulged, and the veins stood out on his face.

"If you wanna breathe, stop fighting."

The teen fought for a few seconds more before taking Boom up on his offer. He went still, and Boom removed his hand from his neck.

After sucking in a few life-saving breaths, KC said, *"Get the fuck off me!"* His features were set in a grimace.

Boom shook his head. "I'ma let you up in a minute. I wanna talk to you first."

"About what, man? Get the fuck off me!" He tried to buck him off.

Boom's hand returned to his neck. "You wanna get choked again?"

KC shook his head. His eyes filled with tears. As he stared down at him, Boom saw KD in his eyes, nose and lips. He saw Solomon in his features as well.

"I wanna talk to you about yo daddy."

Confusion replaced the boy's anger. His struggles stopped completely.

"What about my daddy?"

"You know who killed him?"

"Man, get off me!" The boy began to struggle again, but Boom's position was secure.

"The sooner you answer my questions, the sooner this will be over. I don't wanna do you like this, but I'm trying to figure something out."

"That nigga Hooch killed my daddy!" KC spat. His eyes were red with rage. Tears leaked and rolled down the sides of his face.

"Hooch pulled the trigger?" Boom asked.

The boy nodded. "Yeah. I'ma get that nigga."

"How you gon' get him?"

"I'ma kill him! I don't know how, but I swear I'ma kill that nigga."

"Why your uncle ain't kill him?"

The boy was already angrier than a trapped badger. The mention of Solomon further enraged him.

189

"*Fuck Solomon.* That nigga don't care about nothing. He don't wanna do shit about my daddy. All he care about is hisself and his money. I don't fuck with him."

This matched Solomon's story, and it also explained why KC was living in squalor, while his uncle was living it up on the white side of town.

"What about yo granddaddy?" Boom asked. "Why don't you get him to help you go after Big Hooch?"

The teen became wary. Boom knew he was wondering how he knew so much about his family. But he answered the question.

"Johnny just got out the pen a few months ago. He can't even touch no pistol. He ain't trying to do nothing to get him sent back."

Boom had already decided KC was not a threat to him, but he had one more question.

"You ain't never thought about hiring somebody to kill Big Hooch?"

"Somebody like who? I don't know nobody who be killing for money. Even if I did, where I'ma get the money from?"

Boom nodded and let go of his arm. When the boy didn't take a swing at him, he got off of him completely. Both men stood and stared at each other. KC rubbed his shoulder, where Boom had planted his knee.

"Sorry I had to handle you like that," Boom said. "But you the one who took off running."

"I didn't know who you was," KC explained. "You supposed to run when somebody roll up on you like that."

It was sad to hear that was a fact of life for young, black men.

"Who is you anyway?" KC asked.

190

"That ain't important," Boom said. "I'm just trying to get to the bottom of something."

The teen nodded. Before he walked way, Boom reached into his pocket. He always kept a couple thousand on him. He never imagined using it as guilt money. It was such an unfair compensation, offering it could be considered cruel. But it was better than nothing.

"Here."

KC didn't immediately take the fold of bills. He had never received anything without strings attached. "What's that for?"

"It's for nothing. You ain't never gon' see me again. I'm sorry I choked you."

The boy took the money. He did not say thank you.

"One more thing," Boom said.

KC sighed. "What?"

"Big Hooch dead."

The teen teared up again. His chest hitched. "For real?"

Boom nodded before continuing down the alleyway.

On the other side, Asha was dutifully waiting for him. When she saw the look on his face, she assumed the worst. For the first time since she'd known him, his expression was downcast. She didn't hear a gunshot, but she knew Boom wasn't opposed to strangling someone to death.

He didn't say anything when he got in on the passenger side.

"What happened," Asha asked as she drove away.

"He ain't the one who hired Ben and Jerry."

"You let him go?"

He nodded.

She sighed and asked, "What's next?"

"We go see Johnny."

"That's KD's dad?"

"Yeah. But I don't think he did it either. It's prolly another dead end."

"If it is, then what?"

"I guess I gotta move on and wait for another hitter to come after me. Hopefully he'll fuck up like the other ones did."

Hopefully?

Asha didn't like the idea of waiting for another attempt on his life. But she knew Boom was smart and resourceful. He'd come up with something.

He did not tell her about the guilt money he gave KD's son. Asha was under the impression that he didn't have a heart. He was okay with letting her feel that way.

CHAPTER FIFTEEN
THE FINAL CHAPTER
BOOM!

KD's father lived on the south side of town. Boom thought KC was living hard, but his home could be considered *nice*, compared to the two-bedroom shack Johnny lived in. Asha and Boom noticed a wheelchair ramp connected to the front porch. It was made of wood and didn't look like it was in good enough condition to support anyone's weight, but apparently it served its purpose.

They saw that all of the windows had bedsheets hung up, rather than curtains. There was no porchlight on, but they saw a few lights inside the home. There was no car in the driveway.

"This nigga piss poor," Boom said as he continued driving slowly past the residence. "I don't know how much Ben and Jerry charge, but there's no way this fool could afford to hire them."

"You still wanna talk to him?" Asha asked.

He nodded. "Yeah. Leave no stone unturned."

He made a left on the next street and noticed an alley that would presumably lead to the back of Johnny's house.

Like the last alley Boom encountered, this one was overgrown and intimidating, especially at this time of night. Boom pulled to a stop next to the curb and left the engine running.

"I'ma go check out the back of the house," he said. "I'll be back in a minute."

Asha looked around warily. This was not the kind of area where a woman should be sitting alone on the side of the road.

Once again, Boom knew what was on her mind.

"You know it's a strap in the glove compartment," he told her. "Stop acting like you don't know how to take care of yourself. You a killer. You need to own that shit."

Am I?

Asha had killed two people, but she wasn't sure if she was ready to embody that label. She watched as Boom left the car and worked his way through the dark alley.

In the five minutes he was gone, she contemplated where her life was going. She wondered if Boom would still be a part of her life after whatever went down with Johnny. He had said she would find it hard to return to installing awnings after killing a few people. She wondered if that was true. Asha knew that she had changed since she first met this man, but was it a fundamental, life-altering change?

Before she could make peace with her conscious, Boom reappeared and got back in the car. Asha noticed that his pants legs were covered with cockleburs and other debris. His breathing was slightly labored, but he didn't comment on the obstacles he'd encountered in the alley.

"He got a chain-link fence around the backyard," he reported, "but no dogs. I hopped it and got back there with no problem. His backdoor has a basic lock. Wouldn't take more than a minute to pick it. I'ma go in from there. What I need you to do is knock on the front door and distract him, till I'm inside."

"How I'ma do that?"

"Asha," he said frowning, "I know you new to this, but you ain't *that* damn new. This nigga just got out the pen, and you wearing that sexy-ass dress. You telling me you can't keep that nigga at the door for a few minutes?"

She grinned. "Oh, *distract* him."

"Pretty sure that's what I said."

"Alright, Boom."

"Gimme a few minutes. Let me make it through the alley first, before you knock on the door. Leave the car over here. I don't want him to see what we driving."

"Okay."

"One more thing..." Boom left the car and went to get something out of the trunk. He returned with a holster. "Raise yo dress up."

Asha pulled it midway up her thighs.

"Higher."

She raised it all the way up to her panties.

"Why you showing me that thang right now," he joked. "You know I'm trying to take care of business. You trying to get my head out the game?"

"You told me to raise it higher," she said with a grin.

"Lift your leg, so I can get this around your thigh," he instructed.

It was hard to position herself the way he wanted in the car, but she managed.

He looped the holster around her upper thigh, not shying away from any opportunity to brush her box with the back of his hand.

"Why it's so hot?" he asked.

"What, my pussy?"

"Yeah."

"It's wet too."

"Is it?"

"Mmm hmmm."

"You know you ain't right."

He got the holster secured and told her to get the gun from the glove compartment.

"Put it in there, and then pull yo dress down."

She did as he said and then told him, "This feels weird between my legs. Might have me walking funny."

"You ain't gon' be walking," he replied. "You just gon' be standing on his porch. But niggas like it when a bitch walking bowlegged. You gotta use everything you got to your advantage."

She nodded.

"Alright, gimme about three minutes," he said and left the car again.

"Got it. I'll see you in a few."

Asha left the car two minutes later and casually walked around the corner to Johnny's front door. Up close, the house looked worse than she thought, even under the moonlight. He didn't have a doorbell, so she rapped lightly on the door. She didn't hear anyone approaching, but she heard the lock disengage a minute later. The door opened partly. She had to look down at the man of the house, because he was indeed in a wheelchair. When he saw her, his eyes flashed, and he rolled back a little, so he could open the door fully.

"What's up?" His voice was deep and raspy.

Johnny was bald and stocky, aside from his legs, which were pencil thin. Asha knew he had to be at least sixty, but he could pass for 45. While serving time, she was told that the penitentiary sometimes functioned as a time capsule, keeping inmates from aging as quickly as people in the free world. This could be because of the lack of exposure to sunlight or the opportunity to sleep at least eight hours a day.

Whatever the case, if not for the wheelchair, Johnny looked strong and vibrant. Asha looked past him and saw that his house was neat, but it was very small and very old. Rather than paint on the walls, he still had wallpaper, which hadn't been fashionable since the 40's.

She wore a curious and confused expression when she told him, "Oh, I think I got the wrong house."

"Why you say that?" Johnny asked. His smile was inviting, only slightly perverted.

"The guy I'm looking for said he lives alone," Asha told him. "I should've known this wasn't the right house when I saw that wheelchair ramp."

"Don't let this wheelchair fool you," Johnny replied. "Everything still working down there, except my legs."

She chuckled. "You flirting with me?"

His smile brightened. "I'm trying my hardest. What's your name?"

"Trina."

"What was you and your friend getting into tonight?"

"He said he was taking me to the movies."

"I ain't got no car," Johnny said, "But I got Netflix, and I got some Crown. I can pop some popcorn. Why don't you call him and tell 'em you can't make it? Come kick it with a playa."

"Oh, so you wanna set up a whole date up in here?"

His smile faltered as he looked past her. "Where you park? Where yo car at?"

Before she could respond, Johnny heard a sound behind him. Asha heard it too. She hoped Boom wasn't just now trying to get in the back door. But she looked past the mark and saw that he had already made it inside the house.

Johnny's smile went away completely. Rather than turn around, he continued to look into Asha's eyes as he said, "Is that you, Boom?"

Asha's eyes widened.

Boom placed his hands on the handles of the wheelchair and said, "Yeah, it's me, Johnny. I'ma roll you over here in the living room, so we can have us a talk."

In the living room, Asha and Boom remained standing, while Johnny looked up at them from his chair. The men sized each other up for what felt like a long time. Johnny was the first to speak.

"I knew you was coming."

"Oh yeah?" Boom replied. "How you know I was coming?"

"'Cause Big Hooch come up dead, and then them two faggots stopped calling. You got both of 'em?"

Boom nodded.

"I knew I shouldn't have hired them clowns," Johnny said. "They came highly recommended, but you can't depend on a nigga who suck dick."

"Where you get the money to hire them?" Boom wondered.

Johnny didn't respond to that.

"Solomon give it to you?" Boom asked.

Again, no response.

"You know I'ma go ask him, after we finish up here," Boom said.

Johnny shook his head. "You ain't got no reason to fuck with that man. This here is between you and me. He give me the money, but he didn't want to. I had to pull his hoe card. I told him it was bad enough he wasn't doing nothing about Big Hooch. The least he could do was let me take care of it."

Asha and Boom shared a look.

Boom returned his attention to Johnny. He asked him, "Does Solomon know I'm the one who killed KD?"

Johnny shook his head. "Naw. I'm the only one who know that. Ben and Jerry only reported to me."

"Why didn't you just take out Hooch and leave it at that?" Boom wanted to know.

"'Cause I been locked up for twenty-five years. I ain't never did nothing for KD. Getting revenge on the niggas who killed him is my last chance to honor my son. I can go to my grave happy, knowing I did that."

Boom nodded. "I guess that's honorable."

"What about you?" Johnny said. "Where's your honor?"

"What you mean?"

"You kill my boy and then come after me because I hired somebody to go after you? You don't think I deserve to get you back?"

"Whether you deserve it or not is beside the point."

"*No it ain't fucking beside the point!*" Johnny spat. He nearly lifted himself from the wheelchair in a fit of anger. "*I deserve my revenge! And you deserve to die for what you did!*"

"Like I said," Boom said, his composure maintained, "whether I deserve to die or not is beside the point. You had your chance. You took your shot and came up short. Now I gotta finish this, because I know you'll try to come after me again."

"You goddamn right I'ma come after you again. I got nothing to do with the rest of my life aside from killing you."

Asha was surprised by his boldness.

Boom reached to the small of his back and produced his pistol. Johnny smiled at him.

"Why don't you shoot me in my pacemaker?" Johnny said and began to unbutton his shirt.

Boom thought that was an odd request, but he had no problem granting it. He quickly realized he'd been set up. By the time he saw an electronic device under the older man's shirt, Johnny had clutched it and pressed a button on top. Everyone in the room heard a loud *BEEEEP*.

Boom almost pulled the trigger anyway, but Johnny began to laugh. Asha and Boom shot each other another glance. This time, both of their expressions were wary.

"You know what this is?" Johnny asked.

He lifted the device he was clutching. Boom saw that it had wires extending from it. The wires disappeared under his clothing.

"No," he said, "but I'm sure you gon' tell me."

"This the detonator for my pipe bombs," Johnny said. "I got six of 'em strapped under my chair. This button I pushed just activated them. The moment I let go, this whole house is gon' turn into a burning pile of splinters. Prolly catch the neighbor's house on fire too. You fucked up, letting me grab this thing. You pull that trigger, and we all gon' die *right here, right now.*"

Boom cocked his head, his eyes narrowing. "You lying."

"You think so?" Johnny continued to smile. "How sure are you? If you so sure, gone and pull the trigger. *We can all die right motherfucking now!*"

Boom looked to Asha again. She couldn't hide how freaked out she was.

"Look under his chair," Boom told her.

Asha's eyes widened. She didn't want to get anywhere near whatever may or may not be down there.

Johnny snickered. "Gone and look, bitch. Tell this nigga what you see."

Asha took a deep breath and blew it out slowly. Her heart knocked as she approached the wheelchair and dropped to her hands and knees. She looked under the chair but couldn't make out what she was seeing.

"It's some pipes down here," she reported, her voice trembling. "A lot of wires too."

She rose to her feet and went to stand next to Boom. She knew he couldn't shield her from an explosive, but he was the strongest thing standing in the house.

"What you think now, Boom," Johnny cackled. "What you think now, ol' dirty-ass nigga?"

"I think you lying," Boom said. If he was disturbed by any of this, Asha couldn't tell. "But if you ain't lying, why not just blow us all up now? You want me dead so bad, what you waiting for?"

Asha's jaw dropped as she looked over at him. If he was okay with dying, that was his business. But she wasn't ready to die right now.

"I'm letting you live," Johnny said, "because when I kill you, I wanna be alive, so I can enjoy it. I wanna know I avenged my son. I want to see how the streets react when they find out about it. I wanna live the rest of my life knowing I finally did something right."

Boom shook his head. "How a nigga like you even make a bomb?" He looked at Asha and said, "I don't believe him."

"I was locked up in the feds for a quarter century," Johnny said. "Had me a white celly who got locked up for blowing shit up. He told me how to put one of these thangs together. You might as well quit acting like you don't believe me, 'cause you woulda been done killed me if you didn't. I know you scared to die. Yo bitch scared too."

Boom maintained a bored expression. "Alright, Johnny. What's the play?"

"The play is you gon' get the fuck outta my house," the older man said. "You gon' come back tomorrow, and I'ma be long gone. You gon' try to find me. In the meantime, I'ma get somebody else to take yo ass out, if I don't do it myself. We both gon' be looking over our shoulder for a little while, till one of us accomplishes our mission. *That's* the motherfucking play. What you think about that?"

202

Boom shrugged. "I guess that'll work. You want us to leave now, or–"

"*Yeah, nigga! Get the fuck on, 'fore I change my motherfucking mind!*"

Boom looked to Asha again. She was more than ready to flee the scene.

He told her, "Alright, baby. Let's go," and they left the house without further incident.

He didn't speak to her when they headed back to the car. He appeared to be brooding. Asha gave him time to think. When they reached the Charger, she got in on the passenger side. Boom went straight for the trunk. He remained there for a couple of minutes. When he opened the driver's door, Asha saw that he had a rifle that was so long, it couldn't fit in the car. He had to lower his window and let the stock hang out.

"What's happening?" she asked, her eyes wide.

He ignored her. He started the car, with the front of the gun resting on her lap. Asha's heart thundered. She was afraid to touch the thing.

Boom made a U-turn and returned to Johnny's house with the passenger side facing the front door. He put the car in park and turned off the dome lights. He knelt as he exited the vehicle. From a crouched position, Boom hefted the weapon like a soldier, with the butt on his shoulder. The long barrel hovered in front of Asha's chest, which rose and fell erratically.

Boom chambered a round and stared into the infrared scope.

He told Asha, "This nigga staring out the window. But he can't see me, just the car... You think he lying?"

Flustered, she said, "Boom, I don't know. It was something under that chair. I don't know what it was."

"I think he lying," Boom said. "But we 'bout to find out. When I say go, I need you to hold your breath and roll yo window down. Roll it down all the way. We only get one shot."

"You gon' kill him?"

"Get ready..."

Asha reached for the button to roll the window down, making sure to keep her arm out of way of the rifle's barrel.

"Boom, what if he—"

"You ready?" He was calm, supremely focused.

"Yea, yeah, I – I'm ready..."

"Go."

Asha jammed the button, and her window rolled down. The moment the glass had cleared the barrel, she heard a loud **CRACK!** that was so deafening, she couldn't hear anything at all for the next few seconds.

Boom quickly got back in the car and closed his door, with the barrel of the gun hanging out of her window this time. He looked over at her and said something she couldn't make out over the ringing in her ears. But she read his lips perfectly.

"Got 'em."

They were two blocks down the road when she heard him say, "I told you that nigga didn't have no—"

BOOM!

The explosion behind them was so massive, the shockwave reverberated all the way to the Charger. In the side mirror, Asha saw a huge fire ball rise into the night sky. Her heart kicked so hard, she thought she might pee on herself.

"*Oh my God,*" she breathed.

Boom watched the aftermath in the rearview mirror before turning left and getting the hell away from there.

"I'll be damned," he said chuckling. "I guess that nigga did make a bomb."

Asha shook her head in wonderment. A nervous smile crept to her lips.

"That was the craziest shit I've ever seen in my life. I know I keep saying that, since I met you, but that takes the cake. I can't even believe that just happened."

"Well," Boom said with a sigh. "At least we know it's all done. We don't have to worry about none of that shit no more."

"You, you not gon' go after Solomon again, for giving him the money?"

He shook his head. "Nah. Solomon told me he didn't hire nobody to go after Big Hooch. Technically, he was telling the truth. And he don't know I'm the one who killed his brother... Solomon don't want no drama, after what I did to him when he was with his daughter. He definitely ain't gon' want none when he find out what happened to Johnny."

"Okay...." Asha sighed. "I guess it's really over." She allowed her heart to delight in putting this whole ordeal behind them.

"What's next for you?" he asked. "You ready to get back to your old life?"

She looked over at him and chuckled. "Boom, this is the last time I'ma tell you: I don't want you to drop me off."

He looked in her eyes for a second and laughed.

They drove for another few minutes before he pulled over, so he could dismantle his favorite weapon and return it to the trunk.

EPILOGUE

Asha stared out the window of their beachside resort in Runaway Bay, one of Jamaica's most beautiful islands. The sun had almost disappeared in the western horizon. From her perspective, half of the breathtaking fireball appeared to be sitting atop the water, tinting the sky a gorgeous burnt orange that matched the highlights in her frizzy mane.

Behind her, a beast of a man stared down between his legs, loving to watch the action as his dick slid in and out of her, plunging balls deep with each stroke. As was his custom, Boom was not a vocal lovemaker. But Asha had become in tuned to his body, which spoke volumes, while his mouth remained mute. She knew the pussy was feeling good to him when his grip on her hips tightened, and he drew her to him with each thrust, slamming in so hard and so deep, she would swear she felt him in her throat.

She had never been a vocal lover either, but when Boom was in beast mode, it was impossible to keep her moans and cries of pleasure in check. She gripped the sheets with her arms outstretched, her face down on the mattress, her ass propped up like a sacrifice, and fully submitted to his will. Tonight, he desired to dominate, and she enjoyed yielding to him.

Boom.

He was by no means a perfect man. He was no gentleman, and only rarely did she see glimpses of his sensitive side. But one thing that remained consistent was the way he treated her. No matter how badly she pissed him off, let him down or complained about things she later realized were inconsequential, in the four months she had known him, Boom proved that he would protect her, respect her and provide for her. He hadn't said that he loved her, but he had no problem showing her that he did.

Like now, she could tell by the sounds of his grunts and the claps of her ass against his thighs that he was ready for a powerful release. But he knew that although she enjoyed doggystyle, this was not a position that made her cum. He plunged in hard, making sure to hit all of her walls, before withdrawing and rolling her over.

With her back on the mattress, her chest heaving, her legs trembling, she stared up at her chocolate warrior. Boom was on his knees, his dick pointing skyward, his eyes drunk with lust. The sight of him almost made her cum right then, but her clitoris didn't sing for him until he crawled on top and slipped in slowly and fully. Chest to chest, with his lips next to her ear, he told her, "You are amazing."

That's when she came. She closed her eyes and smiled and rode the wave of their passion, like the sun seemed to be riding the ocean beyond their window.

Boom wasn't a vocal lover, but when he did speak, each word nurtured her soul.

Thirty minutes later, she sat on the side of the bed, bathed and clothed in a new swimsuit. It was a two-piece, navy blue. She didn't like bikinis any more than she liked dresses, but there were a lot of things she'd come to appreciate since meeting Boom. One of those things was the way he looked at her when he stepped out of the bathroom. He was supremely sexy in his swim trunks, but the adoration in his eyes didn't make her smile like it usually did.

"What's wrong?" he asked as he approached her.

Asha showed him the news report she'd been reading on her phone. The headline read: **PASTOR CONVICTED IN BOY'S DEATH BRUTALLY ASSAULTED IN PRISON**. Boom scanned the article for a minute before handing the phone back to her.

He asked her, "How you feel about that?"

She shrugged. "I think it's good, but it won't bring Lil Richey back."

Boom shook his head. "No, it won't. But this is the best of both worlds. He got convicted, and he's catching hell in the pen. This is what you wanted, right? 'Cause it ain't never too late to take him out."

"No, I don't wanna take him out." She looked up at him. "It's better this way. But seeing that reminded me of what happened to my nephew. I keep hearing that one day I'll be able to think about him without getting upset. Honestly, I don't think that day will ever come."

Boom placed a hand on her shoulder and stroked it comfortingly. "It will. If you're not up for working tonight, you can stay behind. I'll be back in a little bit. It won't take me that long."

"No," she said with a shake of her head. "It's my job. I never call-in to work. When you have a good job, I always felt the least you could do is show up every day."

Boom grinned. Tonight, he wore his notorious beard. His hair was cut low, styled in a crew cut. The muscles in his upper body were delectable. Asha knew he'd be the finest thing on the beach.

"Besides," she said, smiling back at him. "After this, we're officially on vacation."

"I feel like this whole trip is a vacation," he replied. "This job is light work. I could do it in my sleep."

"Why you talking shit?"

"I'm not talking shit."

"Yeah you are. *I could do it in my sleep*," she said, mocking him. "So if I fuck it up, what does that say about me?"

"It says you need to go back to installing awnings," he kidded. "But I know you ain't gon' fuck it up. Come on."

They left their room through the patio doors and were immediately on the beach. They walked to the water and then alongside it, hand-in-hand, leaving the perfect set of footprints in the warm, wet sand.

"I can't get over how beautiful this place is," Asha said, looking out at the ocean. "This view could be a painting."

"I'm sure someone has already painted it," Boom replied. "Tomorrow we can go to the city and find it in one of the shops."

"You think a local artist could do this scene justice?"

"You'd be surprised. This is The Pelican up ahead," he said, referring to the resort that was adjacent to theirs.

At that hour, the beach was moderately populated. Asha noticed a crowd of Jamaican girls mingling with tourists twenty yards ahead of them. The girls were bright-eyed, with big smiles, big asses and flat bellies. The tourists were black and drunk, or nearly drunk. One of them had already reached his fill of fun in the sun. He was the only one reclining on a beach chair. One of the girls stood by his side, trying to get him to drink more or smoke more of the island's natural herbs.

"She looking a little desperate," Asha commented.

"Don't let these resorts fool you," Boom said, "Jamaica is a third world country. A rich American man can provide for one of these girls for a whole month. They just need one night with him."

"She should probably move on," Asha said as they neared the crowd. "She's barking up the wrong tree."

"Why you say that?"

"Because the man she's talking to will be dead in ten minutes." She looked over at him. "You didn't think I recognized him, did you?"

Boom smiled. "I hoped you would."

"But you weren't sure. Tell the truth."

"Asha, I wouldn't have gave you this job, if I didn't believe in you. You know how embarrassing it would be to report back that I failed? That's something I haven't done in years."

She didn't look the target's way as they walked casually by him, close enough to kick sand on his feet and hear the heavy accent of the girl who was trying to seduce him.

"You come all the way to Jamaica to sleep on the beach?"

"I'm not sleep," the target said. "Just enjoying the view."

"I have something better for you to admire in your hotel room!"

Next to The Pelican was another resort. Next to that was a dense, tropical tree line that made the area more picturesque and also provided the perfect cover for a novice assassin. Asha and Boom walked past the beach, into the foliage and disappeared completely from sight, as easily as a magician wowing a crowd at a child's birthday party.

Once hidden amongst the vegetation, Asha took their large beach towel bag from Boom. She placed it on the ground and removed the top two towels, revealing a rifle that had been broken down into several pieces. Boom did not help her reassemble it, even though she struggled with the mechanics and got stumped midway through. It took her five minutes to figure out what she was doing wrong.

Boom stood before her, watching her every move. Rather than advice, he told her, "The sun's almost gone."

"I know."

"This one doesn't have an infrared scope. Even I would have trouble with this shot in the dark."

"I know. I'm not gon' let it get dark..."

When she had restored the rifle to its original condition, she took another minute to line up her shot from a standing position.

Boom admired her physique for a second and then told her, "That's a bold move."

Asha started to rebuff him, but she knew he was telling her right. She dropped to one knee and found a young palm tree to prop the rifle's barrel on. Boom grunted his approval.

"Tell me again how horrible this man is," she said as she stared at the target through the scope.

Boom shook his head. "Does it matter at this point?"

"I don't know, kinda." Asha had one eye closed, one eye trained on the mark. She took slow, steady breaths. Her finger lightly touched the trigger.

"He's a murderer," Boom said. "And a thief."

"Did he steal from little old ladies?"

"No."

"Did he kill any kids?"

Boom shook his head. "No. I'm pretty sure everyone he killed deserved to die. Everyone he stole from earned their money illegally."

"Fuck it," she said with a sigh.

One breath.

Two breaths.

Three.

Squeeze on the pause before the next breath...

Follow through with the trigger squeeze.

With a silencer on the barrel, she heard a muted *THOOMP* rather than the rewarding **CRACK!** she had grown accustomed to at the shooting range, but the result was the same. Through the scope, she saw a large splatter of blood.

"You went for the chest instead of the head?" Boom noticed.

She looked up, not realizing he was watching the target with a pair of binoculars.

"I didn't wanna hit the girl with the exit," Asha said, watching the aftermath through the rifle's scope. The native girl was screaming. Most of the beachgoers had yet to realize why she was so upset.

"Bullshit," Boom said. "The exit would not have hit that girl. Just admit it, you was scared to go for a headshot."

"Okay. I didn't wanna mess up my first job. But I accomplished the mission, didn't I? I don't think he's moving."

"Oh, he's dead for sure," Boom said. "Mission accomplished. I'm not hating on you for going for the chest. With this lighting and the silencer, it was the safer shot. You did good. And I must say, you're rocking the hell out of that bikini. I never seen a sexier sniper."

He took the rifle from her and began to dismantle it. "What you wanna eat tonight?"

"Wow," she said as she rose to her feet. She took the binoculars from him.

"What?"

"We just killed a man. Twenty seconds later, you're thinking about dinner."

"Yeah. I'm hungry. But I understand if you feel some type of way."

"No, I'm good. But this is a weird feeling. My heart's beating so hard. I feel like I'ma throw up. Oh, and dick."

"Huh?"

"You asked what I wanted to eat. I wanna gobble your dick up."

He chuckled. "You think it's weird for me to be *hungry* after a hit, but you're *horny*."

She reached between his legs and said, "You are too. You always get hard when I talk about sucking your dick."

There was no point in him denying it. She literally had hard evidence in her hand.

He said, "How about we drop this rifle off and see where the night takes us. Nothing better than celebrating after a successful mission. I can already tell this is gon' be a nice vacation."

Asha felt so too. She watched the results of her first solo hit with the binoculars. Now a crowd of people had noticed the body. They were attempting to render aid. Some were arguing with the Jamaican girl. Maybe they thought she stabbed him.

Asha grimaced. A part of her – a big part – condemned her for taking the man's life. Regardless of his sins, no one gave her the right to be his judge and jury. Asha wasn't able to win the war with her conscious, so she told the angel on her shoulder, *Shut the fuck up*, and let that be the end of it.

By the time Boom had the gun concealed in the towel bag, she no longer felt like an evil person. In fact, she had her appetite back.

"Would I sound like too much of a tourist, if I said I want some jerk chicken?"

"Hell naw," Boom said with a chuckle. "That's one of the best meals in this country. We'd be fools to come all the way to Jamaica and not try the jerk chicken."

215

Asha smiled as she stared into his eyes. They had their hiccups in the beginning, but lately, she and Boom had always been on the same page. They returned to the beach and merged with the rest of the tourists without drawing suspicion.

KEITH THOMAS WALKER

ABOUT THE AUTHOR

Keith Thomas Walker, known as the Master of Romantic Suspense and Urban Fiction, is the author of more than two dozen novels, including *Fixin' Tyrone, Life After, The Realest Ever,* the *Backslide* series, the *Brick House* series and the *Finley High* series. Keith's books transcend all genres. He has published romance, urban fiction, mystery/thriller, teen/young adult, Christian, poetry and erotica. Originally from Fort Worth, he is a graduate of Texas Wesleyan University. Keith has won numerous awards in the categories of "Best Male Author," "Best Romance," "Best Urban Fiction," "Best Young Adult Romance," "Best Duo," "Book of the Year," and "Author of the Year," from several book clubs and organizations. Visit him at www.keithwalkerbooks.com.

CPSIA information can be obtained
at www.ICGtesting.com
Printed in the USA
LVHW091756030921
696898LV00002B/57